LOGICAL MAGIC

ACADEMY OF MODERN MAGIC BOOK 3

MAGGIE ALABASTER

"WE'RE GOING WHERE?" I looked up from my book to frown at Nash.

He had an, "I've got this, don't question me," look on his face, which was as sexy as hells. Of course, it never stopped me from asking before and it didn't now.

"Illusion Bay," he repeated.

"I like the sound of that," Dyson remarked. "Very mysterious." He paused before adding, "Are you sure it's really there?"

I had spent the last hour sitting between Dyson's legs, his arm around me while I read. Apparently reading was now such a dangerous pastime I needed a guard for it.

Not that I was complaining.

Nash shot him a look and Dyson's body shook with laughter.

"Isn't that up near Byron Bay?" Matt frowned. While the rest of us were holed up in a safe house Nash organised, Matt lived somewhere else, but dropped by almost every day. I asked him where he was staying, but he refused to answer. I suspected it was somewhere close, but apart from that, I had no idea.

"Yeah." Nash lowered himself to the chair opposite me. Like Kane and Dyson, he was never far away from me, apart from the odd night he spent away on council business. Or so he said.

I had no reason not to believe him, but he wouldn't give any details either. Some days it seemed as though they forgot how badass I was. On other days it just seemed as though they were trying to save me from stress. No matter how much I growled or asked nicely, neither Nash nor Matt would tell me anything more.

"Illusion Bay is what Byron Bay used to be," Nash added, "before all the celebrities moved in and made it expensive."

"Surf all day, smoke weed all night?" Dyson asked. "Sounds great. When do we leave?"

"That sounds like a strange place for a university."

Kane closed the comic he'd been reading and sat forward.

"Exactly," Nash replied. "But that's where the College of Advanced Magical Education campus is. Amongst the bushes and the beach."

I snorted. "And who came up with that name?"

Dyson chuckled. "What's wrong with CAME?"

I grinned. "Nothing at all, unless you're trying to be taken seriously."

"Life is way too short for that," Dyson replied.

"Hells yeah to that," I muttered. "So, the AMM still has no campus of its own?"

"The council is working on it," Matt replied. He jumped up and started pacing. "They want to find a place away from Zeta influence."

"Right." Last year I was told, by two Zeta agents, that my mother sat on the board of Zeta and the Paranormal Council. So far, neither Nash nor Matt found further information to prove or disprove the claim. I could ask my mother face to face, but Nash preferred I didn't see her, or my father. Until he knew which side she was on, he didn't trust her. Truth be told, neither did I. The suggestion I might be a hybrid had turned out to be accurate after all. What else was true?

"The council is keeping an eye on your mother,"

Nash said softly. "And looking for any connection to Zeta."

I sighed. "It's the last bit that worries me." Why would anyone want their own child to be locked away and bred like a prized racehorse? Did Zeta have something over her, apart from influence? I had to believe they did. I didn't want to think she would willingly want me used in any way.

Dyson gave me a squeeze. "We'll get to the bottom of it, one way or another, okay?"

I snuggled into him more. "I know. It's the uncertainty that's difficult. I mean, why didn't they tell me I could shift? That seems like the kind of information you tell a gal."

He rubbed his thumb over the back of my hand. "My guess is they weren't sure either. Magic isn't an exact science."

"You sound like Kane," I teased. I grinned at Kane, who smiled back.

"Dyson is right, though," Kane said.

"Can I get that in writing?" Dyson asked. "Or better yet, on camera." He reached for his phone.

Kane flipped him off. "Your friend Jess is from a paranormal family and can't do magic. There are no assurances children will follow in their parent's footsteps."

I grimaced at the mention of Jess. She nearly died, thanks to Zeta holding her hostage to get my attention. Nash assured me she was safe, but I hadn't seen or heard from her since that day. She was probably too scared to try to contact me. I didn't blame her. That didn't stop me from missing her terribly.

I shook my head. "I know, but they could have warned me about the possibility."

"Given how hard it is to control the killing urge of the phoenix, they might have been in denial," Matt said flatly.

"Thanks for that vote of confidence." I grimaced at him.

He shrugged, unapologetic. "Why do you think they sent them after us?"

"Because they're pretty?" I asked sweetly.

Matt raised an eyebrow. "They might be pretty, but they're also vicious. You would know that better than anyone."

I suspected he was implying I was nasty in witch form too. I stuck out my tongue at him. He wasn't wrong though, at least about the phoenix. When I had first shifted, I had wanted to kill everything in sight. Only Dyson telling me he loved me had brought me back to my usual, adorable self.

"So anyway," Kane interrupted, "when do we leave?"

"When our escort arrives," Nash replied.

"I assume you're not referring to ones who charge by the hour," I said lightly. "So why an escort? Between us we have two witches, three hybrids, a kickass dog, and an equally kickass owl."

Kane looked pleased at being called that. I knew he didn't think his shifter form was especially intimidating.

"Who's kicking whose ass?" Ariana walked into the room, her boyfriend Hamish in tow. As far as I could tell, they hadn't been apart for a moment since we left the UA.

Nash sighed. "I was just explaining to Peyton that the council was sending an agent or two to accompany us to Illusion Bay. We can't all travel together, there are too many of us to go unnoticed."

"Is this my life now?" I asked, a little snappy at being babied. "Not allowed to go outside without every step being watched?"

"You're allowed outside whenever you like." Nash gestured toward the door.

"The house is in the bush, a bajillion kilometres from anywhere," I pointed out. "There's no one to see me."

"Tell me about it," Kane said, looking sulky.

After a moment I broke into a laugh. He got off on people watching us fuck; the more the merrier. Out here, the audience was greatly reduced, unless we were filmed and put on Porn Hustle. I wasn't quite ready to have myself recorded on camera again. After the photo he took of me was hacked and went viral, I was reluctant to do it again. Although, if I could disguise my face…

The idea of thousands of people watching me made me swallow hard. My core throbbed.

"Anyway." I blinked to return myself to the present. "I can take care of myself."

"I know you can," Nash replied. "Maybe the escort is for the others." His mouth quirked up in a faint smile. He rarely joked, but when he did, he melted my heart a little more.

Who was I kidding, he made my heart a hot puddle a long time ago, along with my sex. So did Kane and Dyson. What I felt for Matt was more complicated. I had feelings for him, to be sure, and I wanted to get him naked and sweaty, but he could be such a jerk. A part of me hoped to see Blake—a guy who had helped me out of the Zeta compound— again at some point.

Yeah, okay, I don't know what was up with me

either. Although we didn't talk about it, I know they all hoped I would choose them some day. The problem was, I couldn't choose. I wasn't sure I would ever be able to. Certainly not today.

"I guess Matt could use a little help." I gave him a sly smile.

"Fuck you," Matt retorted.

"You wish," I shot back.

His tongue flicked over his lips. I was reasonably sure he *did* wish. I knew he liked watching me and pleasuring himself at the same time.

"You know," he said slowly. "You're right. I might need help to keep from getting killed by Peyton or something she does."

I was sure he meant it as a joke, but it stung. There was far too much truth in his words. Zeta coming after me resulted in the deaths of several students and a teacher, the capture of both Dyson and Jess, and Nash was forced to kill again to save us all. I could add a bunch of Zeta agents to that tally. If I went quietly in the first place, a lot of people, innocent or otherwise, would still be alive. I was a danger to all of them.

Eyes stinging with tears, I jumped up from the couch and ran toward the door. I wrenched it open and hurried outside.

"You fucking idiot," I heard one of the guys say behind me. "What did you have to go and say that…"

"I just…"

I headed toward the trees so I couldn't hear them argue any longer.

"Peyton!"

I ducked behind the first set of trees as Kane called me. I ignored him and kept on walking.

"Wait!" he yelled. "Please!"

I sighed and stopped, but didn't turn around. If he did, he'd see the tears which poured down my cheeks.

"He's a dick." Kane was closer now. "He shouldn't have said that."

"It was accurate." I sniffed. "I should leave before you all get killed."

"We're not going to get killed." His hand rested on my shoulder. "We don't even know if Zeta is after us."

"After I ruined their breeding program? Oh, they'll be after me, if only for that. While you're around me, you're in danger."

He exhaled softly and turned me to face him. "I'd rather be in danger with you than be without you." He swallowed audibly. "I love you."

I wiped tears from my cheek with the back of my hand. "I…I love you, too."

His expression softened. "You're the most amazing person I know. And the only other bird."

I blinked in surprise. "Hey, you're right. About the bird part." I didn't feel particularly amazing right now. "Maybe you can teach me to fly?"

"I'd like that." He wiped his thumb over a new tear.

"I'll promise not to eat you," I said without humour.

"That's a shame, I quite like being eaten." His expression was deadpan until I smiled and socked him on the arm.

"I didn't mean *that* kind of eating. That's the kind I can do." I eyed his groin as his pants tented.

"Thank the gods for that." He sounded a little choked. "Maybe we should go inside?"

Honestly, he was the only guy I knew who would go inside for *less* privacy.

A couple of birds called out from a tree nearby.

"We have an audience already," I pointed out. I reached for the top of his track pants and slid them down his hips. His boxers followed, letting his erection spring free. "And he is ready."

"So ready," Kane murmured.

I sank to my knees in front of him and slid my tongue down the length of his cock.

"Mmm."

I looked up at him as I licked my way back up and circled his already beaded tip. Kane's eyes were closed and a faint smile graced his lips.

I closed my mouth around his cock and started to suck gently.

"Gods, yes," he breathed. He tangled a hand in my hair.

I took him in deeper, almost to the back of my throat.

"Peyton, I'm sorry..." Matt skidded to a stop a couple of metres away. "Oh, I should have known." His face turned slightly pink. "I'll talk to you later." He turned around.

"Why don't you stay?" Kane suggested.

Matt turned back, eyes wide. His cock strained against the front of his pants.

I paused for a moment. Matt and I had an undeniable attraction. I might not admit it, but I liked having him around, including during intimate moments. I wanted to explore that with him. Maybe this was our chance.

I slid my mouth off Kane's cock and licked his tip again. "I want you to stay. If you want to."

Matt groaned. "I really..." His hand twitched beside his groin as though he wanted desperately to grab himself.

Fuck this dancing around. If anything was going to happen between us, someone would have to make the first move. That might as well be me.

I moved away from Kane and crawled the few steps across the mercifully soft grass. I stopped in front of Matt and reached for the fly of his jeans. My heart pounded at my own boldness. I half expected Matt to turn and run. This was a big step for us both. In spite of myself, I cared about him as much as I cared about the other guys. I wasn't ready to tell him that, but I could show him.

When he didn't run, I undid the button and slid down the zip. In a moment his erection was hot and hard in my hand. I stroked his length several times before I closed my mouth on him.

He shivered a little. "Oh my gods." Placing a gentle hand in my hair, he guided me down to the ground, so I lay beside him, his cock deep inside my mouth.

I looked him in the eyes and what I saw there went far beyond pleasure, beyond lust. I let my eyes smile, then closed them and sucked slowly.

Kane moved to lay on the other side of me and

slipped my shirt up and away from my breasts. He leaned down to thoroughly lick and suck one firm peak, then the other. He lavished equal attention on both. He was always so considerate in making sure I enjoyed myself.

I rubbed Matt's balls gently while Kane undid my pants and slid them down my legs. The air was cold on my bare ass. I shivered slightly, but Kane warmed me by kissing and nipping his way across my skin. He bent my leg and buried his face between my legs.

I gasped aloud as his tongue tickled against my sex with just the right amount of pressure to drive me wild immediately. Gods, he always knew just what I liked.

Matt bucked slowly and moaned before he pulled away from me. He worked his way down to take his turn at sucking on my nipples.

"I've wanted to do this for so long," he muttered.

I moaned in agreement. Having him touch me felt even better than I'd dared to imagine. Between his mouth and Kane's tongue lapping at my folds, I was already close to the edge.

Kane slid a finger inside me and worked me from the inside and out. Every touch made me want to scream. He played my body like a practiced violinist. I wanted to sing in response.

In moments, I came, crying out so loudly the birds flew squawking from the trees.

At some unseen signal, Kane moved from my sex and back to my breasts. Matt pulled me to him and pressed the tip of his cock to my entrance.

"Are you sure about this?" Matt whispered. His expression was serious, although his eyes were laced with desire. He wanted me, but he needed to know I was sure. He didn't want to see me hurt. That feeling was mutual. I searched his gaze for certainty and found it. He would have no regrets and neither would I.

"Yes," I panted, but was as decisive as I could manage with short breath. "I want you inside me." I pushed myself forward onto him.

He grunted and slid all the way into me.

I groaned with pleasure. He was so damned big I needed to stretch a little more to take him.

Kane, eyes wide, watched for a minute or two, then moved back up to slip his cock back into my mouth.

I took him in and paused for a moment to enjoy the feeling of being the centre of attention for two such amazing guys. How in the hells did I get so lucky? I didn't know, but I was going to enjoy myself.

With both guys thrusting into me, I closed my eyes and savoured the sensation of their cocks. In and out, in and out, in an imperfect rhythm.

Kane grunted. "I'm going to come."

"Mmmhmm," I replied around his length. I sucked harder, took him in deeper, until he cried out and sent hot cum down the back of my throat.

Matt came a moment later with a grunt of pure pleasure and a few thrusts that followed me completely. As his seed gushed into me, I came again, intense and mind blowing, for at least a full minute.

When I finally came down, I sagged onto the grass to catch my breath.

"Does this mean I'm forgiven?" Matt slid out of me.

I suppressed a grin and snorted. "No way. You're still an asshole."

He laughed and opened his mouth to say something. Instead, he stopped and frowned. "I think we have company."

2

I FROZE. After a moment I heard the sound of a car. Distant, but steadily coming closer.

"I'm hoping that's the escort Nash mentioned." I grabbed my clothes and started to pull them on. "Otherwise someone else has found us out here."

"Maybe the neighbours heard you screaming?" Matt suggested. He gave me a lopsided smile so I knew he was teasing.

I stuck my tongue out and pulled down my shirt. "Maybe they heard you moaning."

He laughed softly and handed me my panties.

I leaned against Kane to pull them on and started with my jeans. I had just done up the fly when a car drove up to the house. I just made it out through the trees before I dropped to a crouch.

"They might be friendly." Kane crouched beside me, Matt on the other side.

"The car is black," I whispered.

"Sometimes Zeta drives blue cars," Matt reminded me. "And my mother's car is black."

I glanced at him. That was the first time I had heard him mention his mother.

"Is she evil?" Kane asked.

Matt gave him a dry look. "Of course not. Not that I know of anyway."

I searched his face but he gave nothing away. Since he was a hybrid, his mother might well have taken part in Zeta's breeding program. Whether that was voluntary or not, I wasn't sure even he knew. He might now be wondering how deeply she was involved with Zeta.

I had the same questions about my own mother. I only had a couple of doctor's words that she sat on the board. Unfortunately the not knowing was a good way to let my imagination run wild.

The driver's side door swung open and a figure stepped out. She was dressed from head to toe in black and sported a long golden blonde ponytail.

I breathed a sigh of relief and rose to my feet. Before I could take a step, Matt grabbed my hand.

"She's a Zeta agent."

"She's on our side. Corinne helped me escape from Zeta," I replied, unsure now. "Blake, too." I nodded toward him. His mess of curls shone in the morning sun as he moved to stand beside Corinne.

"Just because someone helped you, doesn't mean they're above suspicion." Matt let my wrist go and rose to stand in front of me. "Are you sure they can be trusted?" He eyed Blake as though he was familiar in some way.

"Are you saying that because you care?" I kept my tone light, but my heart went into overdrive. We had all been through so much, I didn't want to waste another moment on guessing.

He gave me a soft look which melted me a little more. "Yeah, but don't think I'll stop telling you when you're being a pest."

I grinned. "As long as I can keep telling you when you're a dick."

He stuck out his hand. "Deal."

When I shook his hand, he didn't let mine go. Instead, he pulled me around behind him. "Stay vigilant."

I wasn't sure if he was talking to me or Kane, but I nodded and waited for the owl shifter to step beside me. I knew he was trying to protect me, but the truth was he was more vulnerable than I was. I'm not saying owls aren't badass, but he had no magic and wasn't going to rip off anyone's head. He might peck their eyes out though, so there's that.

We moved toward the house as the door swung open. Nash stepped out, followed by Ariana. Her sleeve was rolled up and I knew she would conjure her attack unicorn if necessary. Nash might be susceptible to the gas which put shifters to sleep, so I suspected Hamish would be close by as well.

"Mr Nash," Blake called out warmly.

"Just Nash," Nash replied. "I'll leave the formality to my students." His voice caught slightly and I suspected he was thinking about me.

"Yeah, about that." Blake gestured toward the house. "Maybe we should talk inside."

Nash hesitated, then nodded. He turned toward me, the first indication he knew the three of us were approaching.

Blake looked surprised, but Corinne just inclined her head and grimaced.

"Evidently my cousin needs to work on his secret agent skills," she said, an eyebrow arched at him.

Blake shrugged and grinned. "That's what I wanted to talk to Mr... I mean Nash, about. Amongst other things." He gave me a wink that made my heart flutter. He was too damned cute for his own good.

I smiled and self-consciously brushed grass off my jeans. I probably had grass stains on the knees, but I wasn't about to look. That would be embarrassing. Nope, no looking for me. Okay, maybe a tiny peek. Bingo, grass stains.

I blushed.

"So, I need some tea. Anyone else?" I kissed Nash's cheek as I slid past him and through the doorway. Not having to hide our relationship anymore was one of the major perks of not being at UA anymore. One of many if I was honest.

I hurried into the kitchen and flicked the electric kettle on.

"I could use something hot and steamy," Dyson remarked. He stepped into the kitchen and wrapped his arms around me but kept his hands on my middle. No higher and no lower. He told me back at the Zeta building that he loved me. I said it back. Ever since then, nothing changed. He was still the same cheerful guy who was content to take things slowly. Some day, I'd find the time to talk to him about it. Okay, and the guts. In the meantime, there was no need to rush.

"Coffee?" I offered.

"I'll get it." He stepped back from me to pull mugs out of the cupboards. In spite of all the people who were currently living in the house, everything was always clean and neat. Nash made sure of that. He ran the place like it was a military operation.

We stepped out into the living room with trays of hot drinks, just as Matt spoke.

"I still don't like the idea of splitting up." He nodded his thanks and glared at Nash over his steaming mug. "It makes us all vulnerable."

I looked from Nash to Blake and Corinne, who sat on the opposite side of the room, in chairs they must have pulled over from the dining table.

"Noted," Nash replied simply. "We're sticking to the plan."

Matt scowled, but didn't argue further. Smart move, considering the look on Nash's face. Stony and calm, he was the picture of an immovable mountain. When he looked like that, the only thing we could do was go with the flow.

"What is the plan?" Blake asked eagerly.

Did Matt's scowl deepen slightly? It was hard to tell with him sometimes.

"Do you three know each other?" I gestured toward him, then to Corinne and Blake. I suspected Corinne was a few years older, but Blake was around the same age as the rest of us. If they all worked for the council, then it wasn't much of a stretch.

Matt and Blake shared a glance.

"We've met," Matt replied

"Mathew and I went to school together for a while," Blake said cheerfully. "Before his family moved away."

"Oh really?" I grinned. "I bet you have some great stories."

"As a matter of fact—"

Nash made a slicing gesture with his hand and cut Blake off. "Have your reunion later. We don't have time for it right now. The sooner we're gone from here, the better."

"We weren't followed," Corinne said, her voice tight.

"I'd rather not take the chance." Nash stood and started to pace. "Ariana and Hamish, you know what you have to do?"

"Yes, sir!" Hamish replied. "We're packed and ready to go."

I frowned. "Where are you going?"

Ariana gave Nash a nervous glance. "He asked us to keep it to ourselves."

"The less anyone else knows, the better," Nash

said firmly. There was that immovable mountain again, but I *was* going to argue.

"You're going to keep secrets from me?" I asked in disbelief.

"Not the kind you think," he replied.

"Oh, what kind do I think?" I crossed my arms, which might have had more impact if not for the mug in my hand.

Nash sighed. "It's nothing bad. Will you just trust me, please?"

I hesitated. I did trust him, implicitly, but I didn't like secrets, especially amongst my friends and boyfriends. "Fine, but if it's anything bad, I get to tie you down and spank you."

Nash looked surprised, but then a smile crept to the corners of his mouth. "Deal."

"You can spank me anytime," Kane remarked. He didn't bother to hide his grin.

"I'll remember that for next time," I told him. "So, what's the rest of the plan then?"

"Dyson, Corinne, Blake, and Peyton will travel in the car out there." Nash nodded toward the front door. "Your Zeta uniforms should convince any agents you meet that you've recaptured these two."

"They think we have a score to settle," Corinne said. "After you escaped from the facility we went back and told them we lost you. They think we're deeply regretful." She cocked her head so her ponytail fell to the side.

"And are you?" Matt asked. His whole body looked tense, ready to react depending on her reply.

"Not even a little bit," Blake replied.

Matt nodded slowly but his posture only relaxed slightly.

"Right then. You four will go together." Nash said. "Matt, Kane, and I will be a few hours behind, but we'll take the inland route."

"I'd rather travel with Peyton," Matt said, his eyes on me.

Nash fixed him with a frown. "You usually complain when I pair you up."

Matt shrugged. "Someone has to keep her out of trouble."

"I can do that," Dyson said.

"Me too," Blake agreed. "She's in good hands."

"That's what I'm afraid of," Matt muttered.

"Jealous?" I asked.

Matt snorted. "Of course not." His mouth moved for a moment longer, but he eventually closed it, his teeth clicking.

I let the silence hang for a moment before I broke it. "Is there such a thing as demons?"

Every eye turned to stare at me.

"Demons?" Ariana echoed.

"Yeah. At the Zeta facility I saw a guy with red skin, like something out of a movie." I hadn't been sure I had really seen him, or if I had dreamed it. Maybe I'd hit my head and he was a hallucination.

"Red skin," Nash echoed. At least he wasn't laughing. Yet. "What did he do?"

"He took the stone Zeta was using to dampen witches' ability to do magic. He had two people with him, but they both looked human."

Nash rubbed his chin. "Yes, there are such things as demons," he said slowly. "They are…a shifter mutation, if you like. Instead of shifting into an animal, they can change into a form most of us would find repugnant. A mutant ant, for example. Others are almost entirely human except for some minor quirk, like glowing eyes."

"Demons are real," Corinne agreed. "What Nash said is accurate. They tend to live in inner cities and only interact with their own kind. Some are resentful of the fact." She rubbed her hands up and down her arms. "Some of them would like to step out of the shadows, but their elders hold them back."

"Yeah, but mostly they're just normal paranormals like us," Blake said. "I went to school with some."

I exhaled loudly. "Thank the gods. For a moment there I thought we'd have to tackle Zeta on one side and demons on the other."

"We still might," Corinne said. "The stone they took is powerful. The gods only know what they might want it for."

I cocked my head at her. "You told me where to find it."

"Yes, I did." She regarded me for a moment. "I was hoping to get to it first."

"So you knew they were after it?" I asked.

She looked toward Blake, then back at me. "I suspected they might be. Demons, like shifters, can hide in plain sight. They could have been waiting there for months, hoping someone would do what you did and disconnect the stone from the dampening field."

"They could also have been days away," Blake said. "We couldn't be sure."

"So there's an ancient and potentially dangerous artefact loose in the world," I said. "One that does weird things to witches."

Nash frowned. "It stopped witches from drawing magic. Are you suggesting it does something else?"

I swallowed. "I've been able to draw more quickly and with stronger spells ever since I came into contact with it. I thought maybe it was to do with unlocking my phoenix side."

Nash shook his head slowly. "That's not how that works."

"It was the stone," Corinne said softly. "It siphons off power, but it also releases it. It's taken the power from one witch and given it to you."

3

I GAPED.

"So I'm walking around with someone else's magic while they have none?" I wanted Corinne to deny it, but she wouldn't meet my eyes.

"Is it yours?" Kane asked. His blunt question surprised me. Ever the science geek, he looked fascinated, if a little sickened by all of this.

Relatable. I felt the same way myself.

"No," Corinne replied firmly. "Blake and I are fine, fortunately. We were both far enough away not to be impacted. More likely the stone siphoned a Zeta agent's magic, so don't feel too bad. They would have done the same to you, given the chance."

Even knowing she was right didn't make me feel much better. Having someone else's magic inside me felt dirty somehow, although at least it hadn't done me any harm.

Yet.

"So what would a demon do with the stone?" I asked. "Take magic and keep it themselves?"

"Only someone with the innate ability to use magic can absorb it and use it." Corinne chewed on her thumbnail. "They could certainly make a witch more powerful if they wanted, but that doesn't usually end well."

"Oh good," I said dryly. "Now we get to the part where I'm doomed." I should have known. I narrowed my eyes and her and Blake. Surely they understood the risks before they asked me to shut down the dampening field?

Corinne snorted. "Not doomed, no. Not unless you got your hands on the stone and absorbed a bunch of magic. Then you'd probably go insane."

Matt made a choking sound, as if he was struggling to hold back a snarky remark.

I shot him a look and he made a zipping gesture with his fingers in front of his mouth.

Good call.

"They may want the stone for the same reason Zeta does," Nash said slowly. "To stop witches and wizards from being able to use magic for as long as they live."

"There's another explanation," Ariana said, her voice soft as though she barely dared to speak.

I turned toward her and gestured for her to continue.

"They might just want to keep it out of Zeta's hands," she suggested.

Nash looked thoughtful, then nodded slowly. "It's possible." He didn't seem convinced.

"So they're either a bigger threat than Zeta, or they're potential allies," I reasoned. "I'm glad it's all so clear." I slumped into a chair.

"It would have been handy if they'd stopped to tell you which one it was," Blake said lightly.

I gave him an ironic smile. "Yeah, definitely. It would have been courteous."

"Maybe they did," Dyson said. He rubbed his chin. "They could have stopped to siphon Peyton's magic while she lay unconscious on the floor, but they didn't."

"Right. They stepped around me." That begged a question though. "Can the stone siphon from hybrids?"

Corinne frowned. "It must, since it dampened

your magic, but if they took it, you'd still be a shifter."

"Cool. I couldn't do magic but I could still rip their heads off," I said bitterly. Killing Fitz gave me no satisfaction. At least, not as much as it had then, when I was in phoenix form.

"Being a shifter isn't so bad," Dyson said. He sounded slightly hurt at my words.

I rose and moved to put my arms around him. "Of course it's not. Shifters are awesome. I just… I didn't like my phoenix self. I wanted to tear the world apart and set the ruins on fire. If it wasn't for you, I might have." I gave him a squeeze, which he returned.

"I'm sorry," he said softly. "I keep forgetting that was the first time you knew you could shift. It must have been strange."

"It was. I'm sure it was for you when you were little."

He shrugged with one shoulder. "A bit, but I knew it was coming. The only question was what we'd shift into." He nodded toward Kane, whose face was characteristically red.

Dyson went on. "I was hoping I'd be a tiger."

"Same here," Kane mumbled.

"Me too," Matt said.

Every eye in the room swung around to look at him.

"What? I wanted to be a normal shifter, not a mythical creature."

"Gargoyles are cool," I assured him. "Dragons too," I told Nash.

Nash sighed softly. "It could have been worse. I had a childhood friend who was a sphinx. He kept his normal face even when he shifted. It was…weird."

"But you would have preferred an actual animal too?" I asked.

"I would have liked to be something soft and cute like a possum," he admitted.

I grinned. "At least your human form is cuddly."

He grinned back. "You think so?"

"Absolutely." I nodded. I moved over and gave him a hug. He wound his arms around me and drew me closer still. At least with him I had no doubt of his feelings for me. It went way beyond lust and sex.

"So anyway," Kane interrupted. "Can magic be taken from Peyton and given back to the witch it was siphoned from?"

"In theory, yes, if we could find him or her," Corinne replied. "If they're a Zeta agent, would we want to?"

"Hells no," I said firmly. "It feels strange, but I'd rather have extra magic than give it to the enemy."

"And if it's not the enemy?" Matt asked. "Would you take the risk?"

I hesitated. "Yes, I would," I said finally. "Without it, they're vulnerable."

Matt nodded. "I'll keep an ear out for any witches or wizards turning up without their magic."

"We should all be watchful in case the demon isn't on our side," Nash said. "That makes this travel north even riskier." He was firmly back in his teacher cum bossman hat. There was no questioning him with that look on his face. He was hot as hells, but more than that, he made me feel safe and loved. I would have preferred to travel with him, but I trusted his judgment. Well, more or less. The last time he had a plan, I ended up in a Zeta laboratory.

Okay, maybe I should have questioned his decisions a bit more.

"Maybe we should fly instead of drive," I suggested. "On a plane, I mean. Unless one of you guys has a helicopter up your sleeve?" I looked around hopefully.

"I have second cousins who have one," Blake replied. "They mostly keep to themselves these days."

Corinne nodded. "They do. By the time any of

them checked their phones, we'd almost be in Illusion Bay anyway."

"There are people who aren't glued to their phones?" Hamish said in amazement.

Most of us laughed in reply, but he wasn't wrong.

"As fun as it would be to travel by helicopter, it would make us vulnerable to attack from..." Nash stopped mid-sentence.

"Phoenixes?" I finished for him. "It's all right to talk about them...us. I am what I am. There's no point in trying to hide from it."

He averted his gaze and I realised this wasn't about me. This was about him and his memories. Had he been given the same concoction I had, to force his dragon form to reveal itself? I had several nightmares about shifting since it had happened. And about killing Fitz and ripping off his head.

I reached for his hand. "Are you okay?" I said softly.

His jaw clenched and for a moment I was sure he'd say nothing. Then he gave a deep sigh.

"I think it's time we talked about our childhoods." He nodded toward Matt, whose lips pressed into a tight line.

"Should we leave?" Ariana asked, her eyes wide with concern.

"No." Nash waved his spare hand toward her. "You should hear this, so you all understand." He sucked in a deep breath.

"My mother was a witch. I have no idea what my father was. A shifter of some kind." He pursed his lips. "She wouldn't talk about it."

I squeezed his hand. He offered me a watery half-smile.

"I assume he was a bird of some kind." Nash glanced toward Kane, whose face reddened at being singled out.

"I was literally born in a Zeta laboratory and removed from my mother almost immediately. We were allowed to see each other once in a while, as a reward for good behaviour of some kind." Nash ran a hand over his hair. His expression was pained. Every word seemed more and more strained.

Matt nodded. "It was the same for me, until my mother took me and left." His eyes glazed and I caught him wiping a tear from the corner of his eye.

Nash nodded. "My mother couldn't leave. Or at least, she didn't. I went to school with other young hybrids, where we learnt how we're superior to other paranormals, and why normals need to be brought under control. Every chance she got, my mother told me otherwise. In spite of that, I was recruited into Zeta and joined the police force. They decided I could help them the best there."

He leaned back and closed his eyes. "The more time went on, the more I saw things I couldn't condone. The breeding, the corruption, infiltration of governments, the murder of normals. I couldn't do it anymore. I changed my name and went rogue."

"That must have been difficult," I said softly.

"The choice to do it was easy," he replied. "Actually *doing* it was something else entirely. Zeta doesn't like it when their agents run off, especially knowing what I know."

"They came after you?" Dyson asked.

"Yeah, but I knew all their tricks. The hardest part was convincing other paranormals I was really on their side. Some of us have trust issues." He smiled wryly.

"That sounds lonely." I put an arm around him and rested my head on his shoulder.

"It was." He reached down to cup my ass. "Then I met you and everything changed."

"Yeah, now you're stuck with us crazy folk," Dyson joked.

"I wouldn't have it any other way," Nash said firmly.

"Thank the gods for that." I kissed him lightly on

the mouth, then drew back and looked him in the eyes. "I knew Nash wasn't your real name."

He smiled slightly. "It's the third or fourth name I've had. It was given to me by a friend. He organised the job at the AMM to hide me from Zeta. I'm not sure it's what I would have chosen, but it'll do."

"I like him, whoever he is." I nodded. I turned to Matt. "So is Matt your real name?"

He smiled, but his eyes looked haunted. "I'll never tell," he replied.

"So it's not," I concluded. "Is it Bartholomew?"

Matt snorted. "Gods, no."

"Waldo?" I asked with a smile.

Matt chuckled. "No. Like I said, I won't tell you, but it's nothing that horrible."

"If you say so." I frowned. "I don't even know your last name." Strange I hadn't realised that until now.

"Ling," he replied. "That's all you're getting from me."

"Sure it is." I gave him one of my crappy winks, where both eyes almost closed. He responded with a snort but the sides of his mouth tugged upward.

"We should probably get packed and get on the road," Nash said reluctantly.

I suspected he had other ideas of how to spend

the next few hours. Personally I'd prefer it to sitting in a car for a long period of time, but the sooner we left, the sooner we arrived.

"Illusion Bay or bust," Dyson said.

"Let's not bust." Kane grimaced. He shot his brother a look, then glanced toward me. The message was clear: take care of Peyton or else.

Ah, brotherly love.

"I'll help Peyton to pack," Corinne said. "Otherwise I suspect we'll be here for days."

I blushed, but she wasn't wrong.

4

"Is this where we start asking if we're there yet?" Dyson grinned over at Corinne who sat next to him, in the driver's seat.

I checked the time on my phone. "We've only been on the road for an hour." I sat forward and peered at him over his shoulder.

"So I should have started half an hour ago," he joked.

"Only if you want to walk the rest of the way," Corinne said. She shot him a sideways glance.

He looked to be considering that for a moment before he shook his head. "Naw, I'll get too tired."

I snorted. "If you're lucky, you will. If you're not, you'll be found by a family who decides to keep you as a pet."

He cocked his head. "Right. I could spend the rest of my life lying on a bed in the sunshine and being fed from a huge bowl."

"You'd be fed dog food and might have to sleep outside in a kennel," Corinne pointed out.

"Yep, no ice cream for you," Blake said from the seat beside me.

Dyson groaned. "Great, now I'm craving ice cream. Can we stop for—"

"No," Corinne interrupted. "No stopping until the designated time and place."

"But—"

"Give it up," Blake advised. "You won't change her mind. She's a stickler for the rules."

"The plan was designed to keep us all safe," Corinne replied. "If we deviate from it and something happens, the rest won't know where we are. Zeta would be the least of our worries."

"Right," I agreed. "You'd have to face Nash."

Dyson gave a mock shudder. At least, I think it was a mock one. Angry Nash wasn't for the faint of heart. Though Dyson could handle himself.

"Fine." Dyson sat back and looked out the open window beside him. It blew cold air in my face, but I knew he got carsick, so it was a small price to pay. At least he didn't hang his head out and pant.

"Any sign of the others?" I glanced back, but knew I wouldn't see them. Ariana and Hamish left hours ago, on their mysterious mission. Kane, Nash, and Matt were probably leaving now. I hated the idea everyone was out there somewhere where I couldn't see or talk to them. That left me to worry, which wasn't much help to them or me.

"They'll be okay." Blake leaned over and put a hand on mine. His touch sent butterflies through my stomach. He gave me a soft smile. He really was too damned cute.

I smiled back.

"I know, I just…" Under normal circumstances, a girl might worry if her three boyfriends traveled in a car together. Jealousy or animosity might make things ugly. I knew I had nothing to worry about on that account. There didn't seem to be any hard feelings between them where I was concerned. They might envy the guy I spent the night with, if we spent it alone, but none minded that I had strong feelings for them all.

"I'll be glad when we're there," I said finally. "And safe." I looked back again, but saw no sign of anyone following us. Not, I should add, that I really knew what to look for.

"We should be fine, we're—" Blake cut off when

his phone rang. He pulled it out of his back pocket and grimaced.

"What is it?" I asked.

"It's Zeta," he replied wryly. "They have a job for us."

"They might be testing you," Dyson suggested.

"It could be a trap," I added.

"Um." Blake frowned toward the roof of the car. "I don't think so, but it's possible."

I blinked. "They play games like that with their agents?" Of course they would. Nothing was beneath them. A burst of anger made my blood hot. That was followed immediately by the fear my inner phoenix would burst loose inside the car. I would rip the car to pieces and everyone in it. Then I'd start on the people in the car behind us and the one after…

I sucked in a breath. Forced the fury to cool. I didn't want to kill anyone, no matter the circumstances.

"We're infiltrating them," Corinne said calmly. "We've helped at least a dozen witches to get free and make it to a safe haven. There's a place…" She shook her head. "It doesn't matter now. We're not on their side, and they might suspect that."

"We're absolutely not," Blake agreed. "Corinne is right though, they might try to test us and we can't afford to fail." He exhaled through his teeth. "What do we do about this though? We're only ten kilometres from… Moruya. What a strange name."

"What do they want us to do?" Corinne asked.

"Capture a hybrid," Blake replied.

I frowned. "What makes them think there's a hybrid on the loose in a rural area like this?" I waved out the window. The view was a combination of lush green and black from recent bushfires.

"They found people dead, with marks consistent with a lion," Blake replied. "There aren't any lions in the wild in Australia. Unless a lion escaped from the zoo, which would have been all over the news."

"Wait a minute. You can't be suggesting you're going after this…whatever it is?" Dyson asked.

"If they're killing people," Corinne said. "What choice do we have?"

"We ignore the message and keep driving," Dyson suggested. "Surely there's someone else who can deal with this kind of thing?"

"A whole team of someones," I agreed. "How are you supposed to handle a dangerous hybrid by yourselves? I mean, no offence, you're both badasses."

"We've been trained." Corinne slowed as we approached a small town. "With any luck, this won't take long."

"Those sound like famous last words to me," Dyson pointed out.

"They really do," I agreed.

We rolled to a stop beside a pretty, green park. At the end of the park a wide river ran.

"They hold a market here every Saturday." Corinne opened her door and climbed out. "I've come here for it a few times. Every other day, it's just a nice place for a picnic."

"Are you suggesting Dyson and I stay here and eat sandwiches while you hunt hybrids?" I asked. I followed her example. The sun was warm on my face and the breeze was clean and clear. There was certainly something to be said for living in places like this.

"There's a nice little café just there." Corinne pointed across the road.

"Why don't we all eat, then find our friend?" I suggested.

"Peyton, Nash would—"

I cut Dyson off with a glance. "He's not here. Whatever is going on is better dealt with by four of us than two."

"Or we could take the car and keep driving," Dyson said lightly. "They could catch up."

"How?" I asked.

"Rideshare?"

"Out here?" I waved around me. "They'd be lucky to have a taxi or two."

Dyson hesitated, then sagged. "Yeah, I guess so. But I agree with Peyton. We go together or not at all." He stood like a dog who wouldn't walk past a strange house, no matter how hard anyone tugged on his leash.

Corinne grimaced. "Fine, but we eat first."

I nodded. "I could eat."

"I'll get it," Blake offered.

"I'll go with you." Dyson fell in beside him.

I sat on the grass beside the car and leaned against the trunk of a small tree. "Are we really doing this?"

"Going after a hybrid?" Corinne asked. "We have to. We need to protect the normals. The police can't manage. There are no other teams close."

"How do they know where you are?" I asked carefully.

"We told them." Corinne raised a hand before I jumped up and started toward her. "The most convincing lies are at least partly truthful. They don't know you're here. As far as they're concerned, we're loyal agents, even if we're not the most competent." She scowled.

She was nothing if not competent. Pretending to be lacking just so Dyson and I could escape must rankle a little. I appreciated her ability to put her ego aside to do the right thing. I knew people who wouldn't have done it.

"What happens if they turn up here and demand you hand us over?" I asked. "Neither of us look very restrained."

"I can tie you up, but we know that won't hold you anyway," she replied easily. "We'll just say you came willingly because you couldn't control your shifter form. You wouldn't be the first. Not everyone gets accepted into places like the AMM. Some shifters and witches are on their own." She sighed softly.

"Someone you know?" I guessed.

"Not exactly. Someone I met in the facility. He didn't know how to use magic until he accidentally killed his best friend. A shifter on the police force told him about Zeta. He had his magic siphoned off."

"And?" I prompted.

"And what?" she asked. "He went back to a normal life with a new name and identity, but with no magical means to harm anyone. I don't know what happened to him after that." She averted her face.

"You cared about him, didn't you?" I asked softly.

"I did," she said. "I tried to talk him into seeking help from other magic users."

"You mentioned a safe haven."

She nodded slowly. "Raven's Gate. They train witches and shifters, sometimes demons. Sometimes just the basics, sometimes more. They also train a handful of normals to hunt wayward demons and shifters, but that's incredibly dangerous work for a normal."

"So there are normals who know about paranormals." I frowned. Part of my mother's job was to ensure they weren't able to tell anyone else. I wasn't sure how she did that, I had never dared to ask. I assumed she had them killed, but maybe I was wrong.

"Some are recruited by the Gate," Corinne replied. "Some stumble upon us. Some are friends or lovers. Still others are paranormals stripped of their magic before they were old enough to know they had it. They always feel drawn toward…something, without knowing why."

I thought I caught a glint of tears in her eyes, but she looked away before I could be sure.

I decided to change the subject. "Do you think my mother is really on the board of Zeta?"

"I'm honestly not sure," Corinne replied. "The board is so secretive, I'm not sure they know everyone who is on it with them."

"So, what, they have code names or something?" I was only half joking.

She nodded in response. "From what I can gather, yes. If one decided to betray the others, it could expose the whole organisation and the paranormal community."

"If it was only about them, I'd blow the whole thing apart," I said firmly. "But I care about too many paranormals to risk them."

"Yeah," she agreed. She stopped and glanced around slowly. "Do you feel that?"

"What—" Now she mentioned it, I did and had for a while. Someone or something was sucking on the edge of my magic.

5

I ROSE SLOWLY, hands out to either side. "Can you tell where it's coming from?"

Corinne stood too. She turned her face slowly to the left, then to the right. "I'm not sure. It feels stronger—"

"From there." I pointed roughly to the east. I only knew that because of the position of the sun. I wouldn't have a clue otherwise. Most people don't anyway, right? Well, I didn't.

I took a step in that direction, then stopped.

"Wait, should we be running away instead of moving closer?" I peered ahead. Was there someone there? A couple of someones maybe? I couldn't be sure from this distance.

"Probably," Corinne agreed. She started walking. East. Ish.

"I… Okay." I hurried to catch up, but I kept my arm ready. Or rather, my tattoos. My gargoyle and my tiger were ready to defend me as long as I had access to magic. Here, surrounded by trees and grass, I had lots. Failing that, I could go all phoenix on their asses. That was the last resort, always. I couldn't control that side of me well enough and my jeans were new. I didn't want to risk tearing them. Or worse, losing them altogether. All right, in the scheme of things it wasn't that important, but I *really* didn't want to shift.

A figure stepped out from behind a tree when we were less than a hundred metres away.

I braced myself, but they gave no sign of aggression. Well, except for standing with his legs slightly apart, hand out, palm up.

"Is that…" I didn't finish the question because I knew the answer. He held the black stone which Zeta used to dampen magic.

"Took you long enough, darlin'," he said. He spoke with an English accent. The kind you hear on British police dramas, not the fancy, upper class kind.

I did a double take. I knew that voice. He didn't have a red face now, but rather a handsome one, with hazel eyes and buzz-cut dark hair. His short sleeved t-shirt revealed muscular arms covered in a layer of tattoos. He wore track pants which hung loose from his hips.

"You're the demon from the Zeta facility," I blurted out.

Corinne glanced at me sharply. "Are you sure?"

"Is the sky blue?" I asked.

"That depends on the weather," she said dryly. "At the moment it is."

I exhaled softly. "I'm sure." To the demon I said, "Right?"

He shrugged his left shoulder. "Guilty as charged, darlin'. Don't be too concerned though, I'm mostly harmless."

"Considering you're holding that," Corinne nodded toward the stone, "excuse me for having my doubts."

"What, this old thing?" He dropped the stone into a small velvet bag. Its influence immediately vanished as if it hadn't been there at all. "It's harmless too, in the right hands."

"Your hands?" I placed a hand on my hip and stuck it out to the side a little.

For some reason, he seemed to find this funny. He laughed for a few moments, then said, "They absolutely are the right hands. Why don't you come here and find out, darlin'?"

Before I could respond, Corinne spoke. "Enough of this, who are you and what do you want?"

He sighed heavily. "Someone always has to spoil the fun, and they're usually wearing a Zeta uniform." He waved toward her, but looked at me. "Do you need me to get rid of her for you?"

"No," I said quickly. "She's a friend. She does have good questions though. Who are you and what are you doing with that stone?"

He scratched his head. "Those weren't her exact questions, darlin', but I'll humour you both." He placed a hand on his stomach and bowed. "My given name is Leopold Yarinov Donatello Fitzsimmons, the third. You can call me Leo."

"That's a mouthful," I remarked.

He frowned, but his eyes twinkled. "Leo?"

"No, the rest of it. Can you spell it all?"

He chuckled. "Most of it."

I snorted. "What about the rest of our questions?"

"Ah yes. I thought it wise to remove the stone from Zeta's hands. Thank you for helpin' with that, darlin'."

"You're welcome. Why?" I cocked my head at him.

"Why what?"

"Why did you take the stone?" Corinne said impatiently.

"Would you prefer they had it?" he asked.

"I'd prefer *I* had it," she replied.

"The woman in the Zeta uniform? I don't think so." He eyed her speculatively. "Although, you're not working for them, are you, Corinne?"

She took a step back. "How did you know my name?"

"Same way I know her name is Peyton." He nodded toward me. "The Demon Collective—"

Corinne interrupted. "The collective is a myth."

"Not so." He shook his head slowly.

"Apart from sounding like a show I'd binge on, what the hells is the collective?" I asked.

"The Demon Collective," Leo replied. "It's the demon equivalent of the Paranormal Council."

"The council and Raven's Gate have been trying to make contact for years." Corinne glanced sideways at me.

"By "make contact", she means *eradicate*," Leo said, a sardonic smile on his lips. "Rid the world of all things demonic."

"Only the bad ones." Corinne's voice was tight. "Same with Zeta. There are some decent agents—"

"Like you?" he asked challengingly.

"I'm not—" She bit off her words. "I work for the council. They're not perfect either, but…"

"As interesting as all of this is…" And it was. There was apparently a whole world out there I knew nothing about. I fixed my gaze on Leo. "Is there a point to this? You have a stone which could fuck up a lot of witches. What do you want in return for it? Money? Power?"

"Goodwill?" he suggested. "Maybe I just want the council to back off from demonkind?"

"Sounds reasonable." I turned to Corinne. "Doesn't it?"

She replied through gritted teeth. "Demon Hunters recently thwarted a demon plot to murder all of humankind, normal and paranormal, and take over the world. It's those kinds of demons we can't have running around."

"People still use the word thwarted?" Leo asked. He shook his head. "Yes, those kinds of demons we can do without. We're just as happy to…thwart those. What we'd like is for the council to work with the collective to minimise threats to all of us."

"You want me to talk to the council on your behalf?" Corinne looked wary.

"Oh gods no. I want to talk to them myself. I'm coming on this little road trip with you. I'm sure there's plenty more room in the back. Right, darlin'?" He winked at me.

My silly heart fluttered. I couldn't deny he was charming and I had no illusions that he was dangerous. Any sensible girl would run in the other direction. Me, of course, found him sexy as hells.

"You think I'm going to let you in our car?" Corinne asked.

"I can help you find the hybrid you're looking for." He looked smug.

"How did you know about that?" She shook her head. "Let me guess, the collective?"

"That and he was a friend of mine." Leo's expression darkened. "His girlfriend was killed and he went off the rails. He won't listen to anyone now. So you see, you help me and I'll help you. Everyone wins."

Corinne hesitated. "If I consider doing this, you'll be watched closely. One toe out of line and you will be dealt with."

"Noted," he replied. "Although I would suggest you're in no position to make threats."

"She might not be, but I am," I said. No matter how sexy he was, Corinne was right, we needed to keep an eye on him.

He grinned. "The phoenix has claws." He chuckled.

"And teeth." I bared mine, but he only laughed harder.

I couldn't help it. Before I knew what I was doing, I was laughing too. For the first time since I discovered I could shift, I didn't hate it.

Corinne, on the other hand, scowled. "He can sit next to you then."

Leo stepped over to me and draped an arm over my shoulders. "Fine by me. How about you, darlin'?"

"The closer you are, the easier it is to eat you," I replied.

"Promises, promises. What about you?" He waved his hand toward Corinne. "The three of us could have some fun."

She gave him a look which suggested she'd prefer to swallow a bag of nails and turned back toward the car.

"I guess it's just you and me then, darlin'" He moved his hand to the back of my neck and rubbed lightly.

"How about you prove you're on our side first?" I replied.

"That goes both ways," he shot back.

"Of course it does. We just met." I liked to think I

was trustworthy, but if witches and shifters had been giving demons a hard time since the gods knew when, it would take time.

"And yet, it seems as though I've known you for a long time." He toyed with the back of my hair.

"It does," I agreed. "So…can I ask which is your real face?"

"Which is yours?" he asked without answering.

I frowned. "This one."

"Are you sure?"

"I was until now," I said uneasily. "I'm pretty sure. I didn't know the phoenix was there until the other day."

He clicked his tongue. "Paranormal parents not being forthcoming with their offspring. That hasn't changed, I see."

"Aren't you also a paranormal?"

"In a manner of speaking," he agreed. "We prefer to hold ourselves apart though. No, wait, witches and shifters preferred to hold us apart. Bigots." He looked toward Corinne's back as if she was personally to blame.

She stopped and turned around. "We could stand here and discuss the past, or we could work to move forward."

Leo scratched his head. "I'll take option two."

"Good, then let's focus on the present and future." She stalked away.

"I'm starting to think she doesn't like me," he remarked. "Was it something I said?"

"It might be the magic sucking stone in your pocket," I told him.

"I'm just happy to see you." He grinned.

I laughed. "Are you like this with all the girls?"

"Only the cute paranormal ones who could rip my head off," he replied lightly.

"You think I'm cute?" I raised an eyebrow at him until I spotted Dyson and Blake heading out of the cafe in the direction of the car, arms laden with food.

"Let me guess, they do too?" Leo asked. He made no move to step away or remove his hand from my neck.

"The feeling is mutual," I muttered.

"With both of them?"

"And three more." I blushed.

"You're suddenly quite the bit more interesting than I suspected, darlin'," Leo said. "It seems I'll have to work harder to get your attention. I don't mind though, I'm sure you're worth it."

"I don't know about that." I swallowed hard and moved away from him regretfully.

"There you are," Dyson called out. His nostrils

flared as he took in Leo. "Sorry, we only bought enough for four."

I had no doubt he knew exactly what Leo was. I would have to ask him later how a demon smelled compared to other people, but that could wait.

"Oh, I've just eaten." Leo assured him. "Rest assured, I'll eat again later." He gave me a look which said he wasn't referring to food.

Corinne said something which sounded like, "Cocky bastard," and drew Blake aside.

While they talked, I sat beside Dyson and gobbled down my sandwich. I eyed Leo, who leaned against a nearby tree. In spite of his assurances, his possession of the stone made me uneasy. It made him a powerful ally, but it could make him a deadly enemy. I wanted to trust him, but for now I would watch him and make sure he didn't screw us over.

"It's a short drive," Leo said after a few minutes. "To my friend the hybrid. We should go before he hurts someone else."

I nodded and finished my sandwich. "I'm ready when you are."

Leo wiggled his brows. "Not yet, but you will be."

6

I JUMPED as a bird shot out of a tree beside me.

"Shhh." Leo pressed a finger to his lips.

"I'm trying." I dropped to a crouch between him and Blake. Corinne crouched on the other side of Blake. Dyson stayed behind us.

"I didn't mean to step on that twig." The sound was probably tiny, but it sounded loud in the silence around us.

"Are you sure this is the right address?" Blake whispered.

"Yes." It was Corinne who replied. "According to the message from Zeta, this is the place."

"It is," Leo replied. "He likes his privacy."

The small house sat in the middle of a circle of

grass. That, in turn, was surrounded by trees. The road beyond those was little more than a dirt track. The highway was several kilometres away. The perfect, isolated country retreat. Not my thing at all, but I appreciated the peace and quiet.

"Peyton, Dyson, this as far as you go unless we come under attack," Corinne ordered.

"Then we rush in and help?" Dyson asked.

"No, you get in the car and get the hells away from here," Corinne replied. "Leave this to us."

She rose and started forward. Blake walked a step behind, his expression anxious, but maybe a little excited.

There was nothing like a good adrenaline rush on a Wednesday afternoon.

Leo stood and followed.

Corinne stopped and glanced over her shoulder. "What are you doing?"

"I'm coming with you," Leo replied cheerfully.

"The hells you are," she hissed.

His eyes narrowed. "He's my mate, love."

She gave him a look like she might deck him. Instead, she said, "Never call me love again."

"Or what?" he asked, looking genuinely curious.

She paused. "You don't want to know."

He opened his mouth but closed it and shrugged. "I'm coming with you," he repeated. "You have no authority over me."

"I'm going to be pissed off if you get us killed." Corinne scowled at him.

"Me too, lov…boss." Leo gave her a half bow.

She looked as though she wasn't sure being called boss was much better than love, but she turned away.

Dyson moved over beside me. "I think I've changed my mind about what I want to do when I grow up."

"Oh? You want to join Zeta?" It was meant as a joke, but I regretted it the moment I'd said it. Only a few months ago, I wondered if he actually was working with them. I knew now he wasn't, he was under the influence of a drug they created to control shifters.

"I'm sorry," I muttered.

He leaned over to kiss my mouth. "It's okay. I meant I wanted to be an action man like Blake, but a teacher is better. Safer."

"It is somewhat," I agreed. "Well, depending on the students."

"That's true," he agreed. "Maybe this is safer." He

nodded to the others who were a few metres from the front door of the house.

"If they get in trouble, I'm not going to run."

He grinned. "I didn't think you would."

"I might even fly." As much as I hated the idea, I wouldn't let anyone kill my friends.

"I'll be right there with you." He bit the tip of his tongue before adding, "Have we waited back here for long enough yet?"

"I think so." I stood and stepped out of the trees into the open.

In the same moment, Leo pulled a pouch out of his pocket. He turned to me and smiled before he tipped the stone onto his palm.

"Corinne, Blake!" I shouted. "Watch out, it's a trap—"

Leo raised his hand.

Corinne went for her gun.

I braced for all my magic to be sucked away into the stone. I was ready to shift and tear him to pieces before his friend could leap out and act.

Corinne raised the barrel of her gun.

I held my breath.

Nothing happened.

"It's not aimed at you, darlin'," Leo called out. He

glanced toward Corinne. "Bryan is a hybrid. Without his magic, he'll be easier to deal with."

His words were punctuated with a crash as the door exploded into a thousand tiny pieces.

I threw my arm over my eyes, but lowered it when Corinne gave a cry of alarm.

"What the hells?"

The creature that stalked out of the house was one of nightmares as well as mythology. Head of a lion, six legs which looked like they belonged on a bear, and a tail with a stinger on the tip like a scorpion.

"Tarasque," Dyson supplied. "He probably has a shell as well."

"I'm going to have bad dreams tonight," I murmured, but Bryan was living one. This form was hardly one he could go out in public with. Neither was mine, but a giant bird-like creature was slightly less mind-blowing than this.

"There you go, boss." Leo took several steps back and slipped the stone back into the pouch. "You and my old mate Blake have Bryan's magic. That'll help a little." Evidently that was the extent of his assistance, because Leo backed away and came to stand beside Dyson and me.

"Magnificent, isn't he?" Leo enthused.

"That's one word," I agreed. "Have you tried to reason with him?"

"In this form? No."

Bryan took a swipe at Blake, who jumped back and pulled his own gun.

"As you can see, he's not inclined to be friendly when he's like this. Best stay back." Leo shoved the pouch into his pocket. "I think I might wait in the car. The stone and my own awesomeness was my only defence."

"I thought this guy was your friend," Dyson pointed out. "Shouldn't you try to talk to him or something?"

"I might have exaggerated a little," Leo replied. "We're not really friends. I owe him money. Before you get pissy with me, he couldn't go around hurting more people, regardless."

"Yeah." Dyson looked unconvinced. Something caught his eye and he looked away and pointed. "Looks like Corinne has something up her sleeve."

She pulled her sleeve up and a shape formed in the space between her and Bryan. A moment later, a dragon with silver scales uncurled and launched itself at Bryan.

Bryan roared. The sound made the ground shake beneath my feet. He swung his stinger and caught the dragon in the chest. If the creature had been real, it would have been impaled on the spike and died painfully. Since the dragon was made of magic, it simply evaporated.

It was replaced a moment later by Blake's hawk. The small bird flew in rings around Bryan's head. Every now and again, it would dart in and snap at him with its beak. The hawk did no real damage, but it clearly angered Bryan further. The angrier he became, the more quickly he would tire.

He seemed to realise the same thing. He took a step back and aimed a swipe at the hawk. This time he made contact and sent the bird into a spin before it disappeared.

"What about a gargoyle?" Dyson gestured toward my arm.

"Better that than a phoenix." Although I wondered how well one would work if I created one. The phoenix of a phoenix. I never tried before, although I made a pterodactyl and that was awesome. This was a problem to consider later. In the meantime, I raised my arm and a gargoyle leapt off and loped toward Bryan.

For some reason, Bryan seemed confused by its presence. That only lasted until the gargoyle jumped and tried to pin him down to the ground. He flailed his bear-like limbs and growled long and deep. Huge teeth snapped at the gargoyle and his stinger swiped but only found the air.

"Give it up, Bryan," Corinne called out. "You're outnumbered and out… Out-magicked."

Bryan growled in defiance. He rolled onto his side and dragged most of himself out from under the gargoyle.

Corinne raised her arm and made another silver dragon. It stalked toward Bryan's exposed side as if wary after the last attempt. I knew the emotion came from Corinne, but it almost seemed as if the magical creature could think for itself.

Leo yawned loudly.

"Are we boring you?" I glanced over to him.

He gave me a wink and a smile. "Naw, I just have other places to be. Like on a beach up north. Picture it; you and I skinny dipping in the ocean in the moonlight. All your other boyfriends can come too if they like. The more the merrier."

"I can't believe you're talking about things like that right now," Dyson said.

"Oh? Is that usually your thing," Leo asked, "talking about sexy times during a battle?"

"Well, maybe not *during*," Dyson replied lightly.

"Okay then." Leo nodded. "Where was I?"

"Saving it until this is over?" I suggested. The gargoyle faded slightly, so I sent my tiger out to help.

"You're a hard woman, darlin'," Leo sulked.

"You have no idea."

"I can't wait to learn."

"Leo," Corinne shouted. "Get over here and talk to your friend."

"Um."

"Go on," I told him. "Serves you right for lying about it."

"Ohhh, burn," Leo said playfully. He sighed loudly. "Fine, I'll put myself out there if it'll prove I'm not going to screw you over." He walked forward like a man going to his own execution.

"He's dramatic," Dyson remarked.

"Very," I agreed.

"You think he's hot, don't you?"

"Uhhh."

"It's okay, I do too," Dyson replied.

I shot him a look of surprise.

He shrugged. "The reason I wanted to take things slowly was because I needed to figure some things out. I've realised I like guys and girls." He looked at me apprehensively.

"Cool," I said simply.

"Cool?" he echoed.

"Yeah, cool. Who am I to judge anyone else?" I was starting to lose count of my boyfriends and the guys I was attracted to. Well, not really, but it felt like it at times.

"Great." He smiled, but it turned into a tentative look. "So if I and one of the other guys… while you were there…"

I flushed. My body ached at the thought. "That would be fine," I squeaked. So much for not talking about sex at a time like this. "We should probably concentrate on…um…Bryan."

"Right, yes," Dyson agreed.

The tiger and Corinne's dragon had him pinned. He writhed and snapped, but he looked exhausted.

"Come on, old mate," Leo said from a few metres away. "Give it up, you're beaten."

"Shift back into human form," Corinne ordered.

Bryan growled, still defiant in spite of everything. He writhed for another minute or two, then sagged. A moment later he lay on the ground, a naked, defeated human. His expression was one of utter dismay.

"Blake." Corinne kept the gun on Bryan while Blake pulled something out of his pocket.

"Sorry buddy," I heard him say before he slid a needle into the man's arm and pushed the plunger.

Bryan's eyes closed and his whole body relaxed.

I decided it was safe to get closer now. "What's going to happen to him?"

Corinne exchanged glances with Blake.

"He'll escape," she said finally. "There's plenty of evidence of a struggle." She nodded toward the smashed door. "Unofficially, he'll be stashed in the back of the car until we get to Sydney. We'll leave him with someone from the council. They can deal with him."

"And by deal with him, you mean…"

"Reason with him if possible. If not, that's up to them."

"Bugger," Leo said suddenly when we all looked at him, he added, "I forgot to tell him I can't afford to pay him back."

I snorted. "I think he has bigger problems right now."

"That's because you don't know how much I owe, darlin'," Leo said lightly.

I arched an eyebrow at him.

He grinned. "It's a long story. I'll tell you on the way."

"Yeah, let's get out of here before more Zeta agents arrive," Corinne said.

"Uh, guys," Dyson said. He raised a trembling hand toward the road leading to the house.

"Oh bollocks."

7

"THEY GOT HERE much sooner than I would have expected." Corinne sounded frantic.

"They can't take me again." I backed up a step.

"We're not going to let them." Dyson grabbed my hand.

Blake took the other. "Dyson is right, but we all have to play along with the scenario. Leo, can you carry Bryan?"

"Do I look like a weightlifter?" In spite of that, Leo grabbed Bryan's arm and hauled him onto his shoulder. "What is the scenario?"

"You're assisting us," Corinne said. "As a concerned local."

"That's more or less accurate, love," Leo replied.

Corinne gave him a look, but didn't correct him.

"Best they don't know you're a demon. They won't hurt an ordinary human."

"I resent any suggestion that I might be ordinary," Leo grumbled.

"You're not even slightly ordinary," I assured him.

"See, you get me, darlin'." He grinned, but was obviously straining under the weight of the hybrid.

"Hurry up," Corinne urged. "Blake, get Peyton to the car. Dyson, you too. If anyone asks, you've been there the entire time." She stopped and frowned before adding, "Dyson, you should probably pretend you're drugged, just in case anyone asks. Peyton, remember you're coming with us willingly."

I grimaced, but nodded. I could play along as much as I had to, as long it meant we all walked away at the end of this. Or drove away. Or whatever. As long as I didn't up back in the hands of the bad guys.

The car drew closer. Through the trees a flash of red appeared.

"Does anyone in Zeta drive a red car?" I asked. I knew they occasionally drove blue ones, but mostly they used black, like any evil organisation.

"They might," Blake replied. "I know an agent who has a yellow one."

I glanced at him. "Really? But yellow is such a happy, non-evil colour."

"Unless you're allergic to lemons," he replied.

"Oh, you are?"

He shrugged. "Yeah, anything citrus. It makes my face swell and—"

"Hurry up," Corinne urged.

"Uh, I'll tell you later." Blake opened the door and gestured for me to sit.

Dyson flopped down onto the seat beside me and sagged onto my shoulder. "A drugged prisoner wouldn't sit in the front," he said without opening his eyes.

"Just don't spew on me," I replied.

I looked back as Corinne opened the back of the car to let Leo place Bryan inside. The back slammed shut and Leo moved around to the door.

"You can sit in the front," Corinne said tersely.

"But—" Leo waved toward me.

"*Front*," Corinne repeated. "A Zeta agent should sit in the back with Peyton."

Leo's face dropped, but Blake smiled.

"I'm happy to." Blake swung the door open just as a red SUV pulled out of the line of trees near the road.

Even from a distance, I made out their Zeta uniforms and the general feeling of bad juju.

"Maybe we should leave before they can stop us," I suggested.

"Nothing says guilty like fucking off from the scene of the crime," Leo remarked.

"He's right." Corinne opened the driver's side door, but stood leaning against it.

Blake slid in next to me and held my hand so no one outside the car could see. "I won't let anything bad happen to you. Whatever it takes."

"Me too," Dyson muttered out of the corner of his mouth.

If the situation wasn't so serious, I would have laughed. "You might want to look more drugged."

"Mmmhmm," he agreed.

"Shhh, they're coming," Blake said.

"Agents," Corinne called out. "It's good to see you, but we have the situation under control."

My heart raced as the agents stepped into view. I knew one wouldn't be Fitz, I killed him, but I was surprised to see one I knew. I had nicknamed him Blondie and last saw him when I made a Zeta car crash into a magical waterslide.

"Kear, Davis, and Singh." One pointed to himself, then Blondie, and finally to a black-haired agent.

Davis peered into the back of the car and frowned at Dyson and I. I wished I could have made us invisible, but I had to stick to the plan for the sake of Blake and Corinne. They had to be seen to be model Zeta agents, regardless of the risk to us.

"You managed to recapture these two." Davis waved in our direction. For some reason, he looked troubled by this. I suspected he didn't care for the way Zeta did things any more than I did, but he was still working for them. That made him the enemy, however anyone wanted to swing this.

"We've recaptured the shifter," Corinne agreed. "The hybrid came willingly. You know how some of them are with their new abilities." She clicked her tongue. "Out of control. She was scared she'd kill someone she cared about."

Davis nodded. "Right. That's…sensible of her." He eyed me as if he wasn't fully buying the story.

I gave him a watery smile and nodded. "It's true. I'm very dangerous."

"I'm sure." He nodded and backed away.

"We have the other hybrid in the back of the car," Corinne said. "You can see for yourself."

While Singh and Kear moved around to the back, Davis hovered near the front, occasionally looking back at me. After a while I noticed him including Leo in his regard.

"How's things, old boy?" Leo asked.

"Um, fine," Davis replied awkwardly.

"He's a demon," Dyson muttered.

"He—" I shut my mouth so quickly my teeth clicked. I had no reason to question Dyson. If Dyson thought Davis smelled like a demon, then he was one. I sniffed the air, but couldn't detect anything different. Maybe phoenixes didn't have a particularly good sense of smell, like dogs did.

Leo moved slowly toward Davis. I barely caught him saying, "We're on the same side, old mate."

"Zeta's side?" Davis asked.

"Of course," Leo said easily, "what else would I have meant?"

Davis looked uneasy. "I know who you are." His voice was barely above a whisper.

"As you'll see, the hybrid put up quite the fight." Corinne led the other agents away toward the house.

"Excellent." Leo grinned. He spoke a little louder now. "This will be much easier then. I know what you are. Don't worry, I won't tell anyone. I assume your counterparts don't know?"

Davis glanced toward their backs. "I would prefer they didn't."

"Naturally, old boy. Us demons have to stick together."

Davis flinched.

"What would Zeta do if they knew?" I asked in Blake's ear.

"Officially, demons don't exist," he replied.

"Unofficially?"

He shook his head. "I don't know. Most don't have magic and they tend to shift into…um…"

"Things from your nightmares?" Leo asked, his face just under the line of the roof.

"I mean no offence…" Blake flushed bright red.

"None taken. The average demon has a face only a mother could love." Leo tapped the car roof with his knuckle and stepped away.

Blake swallowed loudly. "I really didn't mean to be rude."

I patted his arm. "Some shifters are straight out of a nightmare, too."

"If you're referring to yourself, there's nothing nightmarish about you," Blake said firmly.

"He's right," Dyson added.

I looked over to him, but he was still slumped against the seat, head at an angle.

"They're coming back," Blake said. "They don't look convinced."

I peered out.

"We'll take the hybrids off your hands," Kear said. "You can do what you want with the shifter, just get it back to headquarters."

It? Fuck you too, buddy. Wait, hybrids, plural? My hand closed around Blake's. A bubble of anger rose inside me. My inner phoenix threatened to boil over and rip the car apart. And everyone in it.

My nails dug into Blake's hand until he jerked. "Ouch."

I smelled blood, hot and warm. I wanted to taste it, to drink it, to paint the world with it.

"Peyton," Blake hissed. "Don't lose control. If you do that, they'll kill you. After you kill us."

I turned and looked him in the eyes. To his credit, he didn't look as scared as I might have been. Blood ran down his hand, but he either didn't notice or he was ignoring it.

"Please, take a few breaths."

"They can't kill me if I destroy them all first." I bared my teeth.

"Peyton, please." He put a hand on my arm.

"If you don't get out of my way, I'll go through you," I hissed.

His eyes widened. "If you do that, you'll regret it. I know how you feel about killing Fitz."

"Fitz deserved it," I growled.

"Maybe, but you don't deserve the pain you'll feel after you harm someone else. Let Corinne take care of it."

I gritted my teeth. For a moment I seriously thought about shoving him away, maybe with a talon. I could have ripped him in two without a second thought.

A tiny part of me, right in the back of my mind, pressed itself forward. Sense, rational thought, whatever you want to call it. It told me Blake was right. It reminded me I didn't want to be a murderer.

I blew out a breath between pursed lips. Control gradually took over and my blood started to cool.

"So you see—" I became aware of Corinne speaking and the agents staring into the car. "We have her under control, but only Agent Jordan here can get through to her. He's helping her to tame her phoenix. I can't guarantee your safety if you try to take her."

"If we tranquillise her like the shifter and the other hybrid—"

"You wouldn't get close enough," I growled.

"They seem to have the situation well in hand," Davis said. "Let's just grab the other hybrid and get out of here."

I resisted the urge to shoot him a grateful look. He was probably just trying to save his own ass anyway.

Kear hesitated, then nodded and disappeared around the back of the car. Singh followed a moment later.

"Are we going to let them take Bryan?" I whispered.

"I don't see that we have a choice," Blake replied. "We've done enough to draw attention to ourselves as it is."

"But…what will they do to him?"

Blake shook his head regretfully. "I don't know."

I sat around in my seat and watched them carry Bryan between the two of them.

Leo stood behind them and scowled. "Careful, old boys, he's a mate of mine."

Kear gave him a suspicious look, but didn't so much as slow down. Evidently they didn't know what he was and didn't plan to find out. They had their orders and they followed them. Bring in Bryan.

I sighed softly. I didn't think things would end well for the hybrid. He'd be used or he would die. Probably both eventually.

"This doesn't feel right," I said half to myself.

"I know, but it's him or you," Blake replied. "I choose you."

"We shouldn't have to choose," I said bitterly.

"I know." Blake gave me a look which suggested he'd kiss me if we weren't surrounded by Zeta agents.

I squinted out at Davis, who looked as happy about this as I was.

"If you need to reach out to the collective, they can help." Leo pressed something into Davis' palm.

Davis flinched, but then nodded. "Yeah. Maybe." He turned and walked back to the red SUV.

"He's a conflicted man," Leo said before he slipped into the front passenger seat.

"Aren't we all?" Blake replied.

"Nope." Leo twisted around to look back at us. "I know exactly what I want." His eyes rested on me. I blushed.

"We should get out of here." Corinne's expression was grim as she took the driver's seat. "We still have a long way to go."

Pressed between Blake and Dyson, I silently agreed. It would be a long, hot drive.

8

WE SLID until the southern suburbs of Sydney about fours later, without any sign of anyone following us. Granted, the closer we got to the city, the thicker the traffic was. We could have a dozen cars on our tails and not realise it. Fortunately the heavier the traffic, the less chance of Zeta trying anything nasty. At least, that was what I told myself. That hadn't stopped them from coming after us in Melbourne.

"So, what happens now?" Dyson asked. He stretched and yawned, his fake sleep having turned into a real one a couple of hours ago.

"Oh good, you've stopped snoring," Leo said from the front seat.

"I do not snore," Dyson protested.

Leo turned around and gave him a wink.

Dyson cocked his head like a dog and let his tongue loll out to the side.

I giggled, but he brought up a good question. "You're not actually planning to take us to Zeta headquarters?" Although maybe I could let my inner phoenix loose there. No, I didn't want to kill, but they might leave us alone if I toyed with them a bit.

Rational thought caught up a moment later. They also had phoenixes and those shifters probably knew how to tear off heads better than I did. I didn't relish the idea of getting us all killed.

"No, this is where you escape," Corinne replied. "But Blake is going to go with you. Officially, you charmed him into your way of thinking."

I eyed Blake sideways. "And unofficially?"

He blushed. "It might be true," he admitted. "I've decided to continue to study at the AMM."

"Oh." My mouth stayed in that shape for a few moments. "I didn't know you'd gone there?"

He shrugged. "A couple of years ago. I left to help Corinne with Zeta, but I think my place is there now."

"Peyton has that effect on people, doesn't she?" Dyson asked softly.

"Yeah," I muttered. "It's all fun and games until you decide I have to choose between you."

"Bah." Leo waved dismissively. "Who needs to make a choice like that? Plenty of folks live in polyamorous relationships."

"By "folk" do you mean it's normal in demon circles?" Blake asked, genuine curiosity on his face.

"Demons, normals, paranormals, hippies." Leo smiled.

"Hippies?" I echoed.

"Sure, why not? They're all about free love and all that."

I glanced at Blake who looked amused. "So what will you study?"

Dyson was studying primary education, I was studying high school teaching and Kane was doing science. Matt was a computer science major and a bigger geek than he looked. Luckily, I liked geeks.

"Biomedical engineering," Blake replied. "It's hard for shifters to work with prosthesis because they can't change them along with the rest of their bodies. I was hoping to find a way to do that. Maybe with engineering, maybe with magic."

"You, old boy, might be the biggest geek I have ever met," Leo remarked. In spite of his words, he sounded impressed.

"That's because you haven't met Kane," Dyson said. "He runs geek rings around the rest of us."

"He really does," I agreed. "Although Matt isn't far behind." *And has an adorable behind.* I sighed, then turned back to Blake. "I'm impressed. That sounds amazing."

"Thanks," he murmured. "We're nearly there."

I glanced out the window. To my surprise we were deep in the city now. The suburbs gave way to…well, higher density suburbs. Those sat side by side with various businesses in a mishmash of styles and states of repair.

"We'll be dropped off at the train and make our way from there." Blake handed out train cards to Dyson and I. When Leo held out his hand, Blake simply looked at it for a moment. "Sorry, old boy, we weren't anticipating you. Besides, aren't you stopping in Sydney?"

"Ahhh, no. I got into some trouble with a couple of Demon Hunters here. It's best I avoid them."

"It's a big city," Corinne remarked.

"I have a big personality," Leo said proudly.

"We've noticed," she agreed. "We're not taking any responsibility for you."

"Great," Leo grinned. "Then no one will mind if I tag along."

"I don't mind," I said.

"Me either," Dyson added.

Blake hesitated. "Fine, but I still don't have a train card for you." He slipped off his Zeta shirt and pulled out a blue one from a bag next to his feet.

Before he tugged it on over his head, I took a moment to admire his physique. Of course he had to be fit to work for Zeta, so he was toned in all the right places. A sprinkling of hair covered his chest, the same colour as that on his head and just as curly. I wanted to run my hands over it, to tangle my fingers in those curls. As for his lickable abs, well… they looked extremely lickable.

To my disappointment he pulled down his shirt. "There's not enough room to change my pants, but I look a lot less Zeta-ish now."

"Yes, you do," I replied. "Much more 'starving student', like the rest of us." I raised an eyebrow at the holes in his shirt, but I smiled to show I was teasing. He needed to look normal now, unobtrusive, and he did. Well, as much as he could when he was still as cute as hells. There wasn't much we could do about that, except go invisible. In a place as crowded as this, that wasn't always a good option, but we'd do it if necessary.

"That's what I was going for," he replied, a dimple forming in his cheek. "My parents would be so proud."

"They like scruffy?" Dyson asked, teasing as well.

Blake grinned, but it faded after a moment. "They like well-educated. They were disappointed when I dropped out. Especially when they found out why." He grimaced.

I winced. "Not the future they hoped for their young wizard?"

"Not so much," he agreed. "They're no fans of Zeta and were even less thrilled at the risk Corinne had dragged me into."

"Hey, you were a willing participant," she said over her shoulder.

"Consensual espionage is so much sexier," Leo remarked.

"Consensual anything," I agreed.

"Absolutely." He nodded.

"All right folks, here's where you get off." Corinne pulled the car into a parking space.

"What are you going to do?" I asked. She was more than capable of looking after herself, but she would still be alone, without any of us to help her if she needed it.

"I'll see you in a few weeks," she replied evenly. In spite of her calm, her voice wavered a little.

"Come with us now," I urged. "We can all just

disappear off Zeta's radar." Nash did it. Matt too. Corinne could make a new life in Illusion Bay.

"I can't." She shook her head. "There are still paranormals who need my help. I won't abandon them." She got out of the car and started to pull bags out of the back.

Before I could move to help, Blake put a hand on my arm.

"She's made up her mind," he said. "Trust me, I've tried to change it. She's one stubborn witch."

"I heard that," she called out.

"You were supposed to," he called back. He pushed the door open and climbed out. I followed close behind.

"Hey, darlin', what do you say we ditch this lot and get lost in the crowds ourselves?" Leo jerked a thumb toward the others.

"Tempting," I replied dryly, "but I'll pass. You can come with us or not, but I'm going with them." I raised an eyebrow at him. I hoped he did decide to travel with us, partly because I enjoyed his company and partly because he still had the stone. I'd like to learn more about it, but more than that, I wanted to be sure it was in safe hands. That, as far as I was concerned, was ours. Yeah, okay, there probably were more qualified people to deal with it, but we were doing the best we could. Besides, Nash and Matt would have a better idea than anyone what to do with the stone.

"I wouldn't dream of being anywhere else, darlin'," Leo replied. "Besides, you need me."

"How do you figure that?" Corinne asked. She handed me my bag and closed the back of the car.

"Because I'm me, love, that's why," he replied. He stepped toward the sidewalk with a swagger.

"Are all demons as cocky as you?" I asked.

"Only the handsome ones." He gave me a wink that set my heart racing.

"It's kinda hot," Dyson said.

"Isn't it though, big boy?" Leo wiggled his eyebrows. He grabbed my hand with one of his and Dyson's in the other. "Come on, Curly," he said to Blake over his shoulder before he started to march toward the train station.

Blake shook his head and trotted to keep up.

I glanced back in time to see Corinne pull the car away from the curb. I nodded to her, but wasn't sure if she saw or not. I worried at my lip with my teeth.

"She'll be okay," Blake assured me. "She'll turn up in a week or two, probably with a few witches in tow. She won't rest until she saves the world."

Or dies trying, I added mentally.

"I know. She's pretty amazing, that cousin of yours." I clasped his hand in my spare one and gave it a squeeze.

"She really is. She's been like a sister to me." He gave me a squeeze back, but didn't let go until the crowds became too thick to walk in a line like we were.

The moment I let go of him and Leo, the crowds surged forward and pushed me with them.

I looked back, but only caught sight of Dyson's face in the press. He mouthed something, but I couldn't make it out as I was pushed forward again. I tried to stop and stand in place, but the crush of people almost dragged me off my feet.

I suppressed the urge to shift and tear my way back to the guys. That wouldn't be particularly subtle.

Instead, I went with the flow. They were carrying me toward the train platform anyway. Once there, I just had to find platform fourteen—no three quarters—and wait for the guys. All while hoping Leo didn't decide to choose now to show his demon face. That would clear the station in a matter of moments, but would also be lacking in the subtlety department. I suspected subtle wasn't his strong suit, but we needed it today.

The crowds thinned as I reached platform one. No doubt fourteen was right at the other end. Typical.

I glanced around, but saw no sign of any of the guys. I chewed my lip again, but started to weave through people toward the higher numbered platforms. Three, four, five.

I spied a doorway with a sign above it reading, "Through to platforms ten to fifteen

Figures, I was in totally the wrong place and according to the screen beside the sign, the train would arrive in less than two minutes.

"Fuck," I muttered under my breath.

I hurried forward and almost tripped over someone's bag.

"Double fuck."

"Watch where you're going," an older woman snapped. She brushed my arm in her haste to grab up the bag and hold it to her.

I would have argued, but the screen now said the train would arrive in under a minute.

"Sorry." I shot her a smile and continued toward the other end of the station at a trot.

Platform ten, eleven.

I ran a little faster, my bag bouncing on my back with each step.

Twelve.

Thirteen.

I spied fourteen just up ahead and sprinted around a group of school kids.

Shit.

There was the train. Where were the guys?

I skidded to a stop on platform fourteen just as the train door slid shut and the train pulled away.

Through the window I saw the frantic faces of Blake and Dyson.

I mouthed, "I'll catch up to you," and gave them a wave before they were drawn out of sight.

Fucking fuckity fuck!

"It's okay," I said under my breath. "The next train will leave..." I checked the board. "Tomorrow morning."

Crap.

I moved back from the edge of the platform and leaned against a pillar. I could call Corinne and ask her to come back and get me, but she'd taken enough risks on my behalf. I couldn't ask her to take another.

I winced at the idea of calling Nash and seeing how far away the guys were. He would come and get me, but he might tear Blake and Dyson a new one for leaving me stranded. Although it wasn't their fault, he would still be pissed. They must have assumed I'd boarded the train before they did.

No, it would be better to find somewhere to wait, and catch up in the morning. With any luck, I'd arrive in Illusion Bay before Nash. I admit, I also wanted to arrive before Matt. If I didn't, I would probably never hear the end of it. As much as I adored him, he would never stop giving me hells. That was just as well, since I didn't plan on stopping any time soon either.

Okay, I better find a hotel then. I pulled out my phone and shot off a text to Dyson so he knew my plan. He responded a moment later with a string of sad face emojis and a thumbs up. There was nothing he or Blake could do but ride the train to its destination.

"There you are, darlin'. I guess I'm not the only one who missed the train, eh?" Leo's cheerful voice jerked me out of my thoughts. He held a train card in one hand and a newspaper in the other.

"I didn't know people still read those in paper form," I remarked.

He shrugged. "Something to do on the long train ride. I guess I'll save it for later." He tucked it under one arm and pushed the train card into his pocket. "Come on then." He turned and headed toward the exit.

"Where are we going?" I asked, without taking a step to follow him.

"I have a mate who lives hereabouts. He'll let us stay there and give us a feed. Don't worry, he won't bite."

"What about you?" I tried not to look as if I was looking toward the pocket where he stashed the stone. He could do a lot more than bite if he wanted to.

He stopped and looked back at me. "I'm not going to hurt you, I swear on my mother's life."

"Is she still alive?"

He hesitated, then broke into a smile. "No, she's not, but if she was, I would swear on it."

"Right." I eyed him sideways. Call me a cynic, but I wasn't entirely convinced.

He stepped back toward me, his gaze locked on mine. For those few seconds, the world melted away and it was just us. A witch-hybrid phoenix and a demon of dubious integrity but undeniable charm.

"What if I *want* you to bite me?" I asked.

His grin was back. "Then I'd bite you as hard as you want, darlin'. For the record, I don't mind a few teeth marks here and there. Now, come on. I don't know about you, but I'm ravenous. My mate does the best pizza you've ever had. Guaranteed."

My ears perked up at that. "Pizza, you say?"

"I do say," he agreed.

"Best ever, hmmm? That's a pretty high yardstick. I've had some epic pizza."

"Not like this, you haven't. It'll make you come back for more until we have to be rolled out the door. Don't worry though, we can work it off afterward." There he went, winking again.

"Fine, you had me at pizza." I pushed my bag up my shoulder.

"Pizza, the real universal language of love," he said with a dramatic gesture which almost connected with the face of an unsuspecting commuter. "Oops, sorry."

The commuter glared at Leo, but hurried on as a train drew into platform thirteen.

I smothered a laugh with my hand and hurried to catch up with Leo.

"I think we're supposed to be keeping a low profile," I reminded him.

"I never have been very good at doing that," he admitted. "That's why I have debts and Demon Hunters chasing after me. I tend to stick out, even with this face."

I couldn't argue with that. He was tall, handsome, and covered in more tattoos than bare skin. Guys like him tended to draw the eye. His accent and personality cemented him in my memory at least. I wondered what he was into, although at the moment I really needed to worry more about getting to somewhere Zeta wouldn't find us.

"For both of our sakes, try," I told him. "I'm not going back to a lab." I flushed at remembering the first time he saw me was when I was lying naked on the floor, having finally shifted back to human form. As far as I could recall, he hadn't stopped for a look, or anything else, but I was still embarrassed.

"Not going to happen," he said firmly. "Not on my watch. I have more than a few tricks up my sleeve."

"Me too, I guess." I was, after all, still a witch. I could tear the place apart with magic if I wanted to. Better yet, I could go invisible. That might go unnoticed now, with people hurrying past to catch trains or go about their daily…whatever they had to do. I would put that on the maybe pile for now. At the moment I felt safe enough. That is to say, I saw no one in a Zeta uniform.

Yet.

"Of course you do," he assured me. "You're a badass. I knew that the moment I lay eyes on you. That was in your phoenix form, by the way."

"How did you even get in there?" I asked. "Zeta

should have the best security the government can afford."

"And then some, given the current government," he replied dryly. "Corinne and Blake aren't the only ones working things from the inside."

"Let me guess, you had a mate there?" I remembered he hadn't been alone.

"Something like that," he agreed. "I called in a favour."

"It must have been a big one, to get you into a place like that." Personally, when I was in there, I could only think about getting out. I couldn't imagine wanting to go back on purpose.

"It's always a big one. Go hard or go home."

"That stone must be important for you to take the risk of going in to get it. I assume Zeta would kill you if they knew what you are?"

He stopped and regarded me for a moment. "You don't pull any punches, do you, darlin'? If you want the stone, you only have to ask."

I hesitated for a moment. "Maybe not out here, surrounded by people."

He gave a curt nod and resumed walking. "For the record, yes, they would have killed me. My witch friend made us invisible for most of our harrowing journey through the building. To be fair, though, they would kill me because I'm me, regardless of my other face."

"You've pissed Zeta off in the past?" I guessed. Who hadn't he gotten on the wrong side of?

"I have a tendency to turn up in the wrong place and relieve them of items they believe are theirs," he said easily.

"There are more stones like that?" I don't know why I found that surprising, but I did.

"Loads. And they all do different things, depending on the magic put into them. Some control the minds of normals. Some can do the opposite and protect the wearer from mind control. Those are tricky, they let the wearer see right through an invisibility bubble. I heard of one used to trap demons inside." He shuddered.

I glanced over at him. "Trapped? How?"

"Trapped," he repeated. "As in, their consciousness is transferred inside." He waved a hand. "It's a long story for another time. We should hurry, I'd hate to be recognised out here."

"Are you really that notorious?" I asked, half teasing. I wasn't sure if he was just playing up to the role of badass demon.

"And then some." He grinned. "I like to live on the edge, it makes life more exciting."

"Hmmm," I said thoughtfully. "It seems I might be safer away from you then."

"Possibly," he agreed, "but then you wouldn't get pizza."

I pulled a face. "Fine, but this mate of yours better not want you dead as well."

"Oh no, not at all. He would probably like to see me inconvenienced, but not dead."

I snorted. "Is that much better?"

"Definitely." Leo nodded. "Death is usually a bit more permanent."

"Usually?"

"I know some demons who can reattach their own heads. Their brains are in their chests."

"That's an interesting place to keep it."

"Right? I keep mine in my groin."

I laughed. "I didn't doubt it for a moment."

"It just means my dick is smarter than average. It knows just what the ladies like." He wiggled his brows and gave me a cocky smile.

"Does it now?" Of course now my eyes had to go there.

"So they say," he replied. "But you're welcome to find out for yourself."

"Has anyone told you you're very forward?"

"If an adjective exists, it's probably been used to

describe me." He stopped at the edge of the road and waited for the traffic light to change. "I prefer to concentrate on the positive ones. You know, handsome, intelligent, articulate…"

"Modest." I smiled.

"Never that," he said. "Life is too short not to embrace your best qualities." He eyed my breasts.

"Right." I licked my lips. "How far to this pizza place?"

"Just another few minutes walk." He nodded ahead of us. "A word of warning though. Johan's place is a little…different."

"Different how?" What could be more strange than anything I already saw over the last couple of years?

"It's… You'll see." He led me up the street to an alley. He stopped at a faded red door and tapped on it three times.

"Best kept secret in the city," Leo explained. "Johan's Pizza."

Hidden as it was, I didn't know how it was still in business. It wasn't the kind of place you'd stumble on while walking around looking for dinner. No sign suggested a restaurant, or a business of any kind, operated here.

The door swung open. The smells which rushed

out contradicted my assumptions. My mouth watered immediately.

"Leo." The tall man who had opened the door looked unimpressed to see him.

"Johan, my old mate." Leo stepped forward and tugged me inside. "It's been a long time."

"Not long enough." Still, Johan stepped back and closed the door behind us. He gave me a quick look and a nod before he bustled away.

"He's not the chatty type," Leo said.

"You think?" I followed them down a short corridor and into a wide courtyard. Surrounded on four sides by buildings, none of which had windows on this side, the residents probably didn't even know it was there.

Paranormals sat at various tables around the courtyard. A couple had green faces and long noses. Another had a round face and reddish fur. Several looked like normal humans, but I would have bet anything they were demons or shifters, maybe witches or wizards.

"Welcome to Johan's. Paranormals only allowed," Leo placed his bag against the wall.

"I can't believe you'd step foot in here." A man almost as wide and he was tall rose from his chair and launched himself at Leo.

10

LEO STEPPED ASIDE and the man staggered past a few steps.

"Gregor, you old fucker," Leo said cheerfully. He ducked as Gregor turned and swiped a meaty fist at his head. "They love me here, as you can see."

"Evidently." I stepped a safe distance away, although I could have had Gregor on his stomach, his arm twisted up behind him in a heartbeat if I wanted to. Failing that, my inner phoenix could tear him in two. "Do you owe him money too?"

"No, Gregor is an old friend from childhood. He's jealous of my good looks."

Gregor grunted. "This man is a double-crossing piece of crap. Told the Demon Hunters where to find me. They wouldn't leave me alone for weeks."

"Oh," I said slowly, "I guess that's bad."

"I'm not even a demon," Gregor growled. "I'm pure, law-abiding shifter."

Leo clicked his tongue. "Law-abiding? That's a stretch." He glanced toward me. "Gregor runs an auction house. Let's just say some of his goods are not legally obtained."

"Where the seller gets their goods is none of my business," Gregor muttered. "I just sell 'em."

"That amulet was mine," Leo said reasonably. "Stolen by some low life and sold by you." He poked a finger in Gregor's direction.

"Who did you steal it from?" Gregor asked.

Leo smiled, but didn't deny the accusation. "That's beside the point, old boy."

"It sounds as if you're as bad as each other." I slipped into a chair and picked up the menu.

"I dunno why I let either of them in." Johan slid up to the table, order pad in hand.

"I was wondering the same thing," I agreed. At least Gregor had stopped trying to beat up Leo. For now. "Can I please get a pizza with everything except anchovies, and a glass of red wine."

"Everything?" Johan echoed. "Including the crickets, banana, and tuna?"

I blinked.

He shrugged. "We have a varied clientele here."

"Right." I checked the menu and chose a pizza with all the regular toppings before handing the menu to Johan.

He backed away and disappeared through a doorway as Leo sat beside me.

"Banana on pizza?" I whispered.

He grinned. "Don't knock it until you try it."

I grimaced. "Hard pass."

"It's not as tasty as the tuna," he agreed.

I opened my mouth to comment, but closed it again. For all I knew, tuna really was delicious, but I'd leave it for sandwiches and sushi.

"So whose amulet was it?" I asked finally.

"I was wondering how long it would take you to ask." He sighed. "It's a long story."

"We have a few hours to spare."

"And you won't let up until I tell you, I assume?"

"Exactly." I propped my elbows on the table. "Come on then, spill."

"Fine. It originally belonged to a member of the collective."

"Is it sensible to steal from one of them?" I asked. Taking anything from people with power didn't seem like it would end well.

"Of course not," he replied, "but they were

corrupt. Tried to take over the collective and bring all the demons under their control. The amulet projected them from attack. They needed someone sneaky to get it so they could get him."

"And did they?"

"Not without a fight, but in the end they did."

"Thanks to you."

He puffed out his chest. "Yes, exactly."

"Because you're a sneaky, dishonest thief," I teased.

He pouted. "If you want to call me that. I prefer to be thought of as an undercover operative."

I waited.

"I like to get under the covers as often as possible."

And there it was. I rolled my eyes playfully. "Does your charm usually get you what you want?"

"Not nearly as often as I'd like," he admitted. "But maybe I just needed to wait for the right situation."

"And you think that involves me?"

He looked thoughtful. "I'm almost certain of it. You like me, I like you…"

"You're sure I like you?" I asked.

He pouted again. "I'm reasonably certain. I am very likeable."

I found myself taking his hand. "I do like you," I

assured him. "My situation is complicated. Not everyone is going to want to get themselves involved in anything so—"

"Fascinating?" he suggested. "Compelling? Sexy?"

I gaped for a moment. "All of those things. It's anything but straightforward."

"That's okay, I'm anything but straight. And straightforward is boring. You can't tell me your life is that."

"Boring? No, it certainly isn't. Sometimes I wish it was, but I don't see that happening anytime soon."

He stroked the back of my hand with his thumb. "We can take some time tonight to make things normal for a bit. We can eat, drink and enjoy each other's company."

"With Gregor glaring at you from his table." I nodded toward Gregor and wondered what he could shift into. The size of a shifter's human form didn't dictate what they could become, or I'd guess bear or elephant. He was just as likely to become a chihuahua.

"We could always go somewhere else to be alone," Leo suggested.

"Maybe after we eat." I was starving.

I pulled my phone out of my pocket as it

vibrated. "Text from Dyson." I shot one back to assure him I was fine and ask how he was.

A moment later I got one from Blake with much the same question. I replied in the same way.

After a few seconds I got another from Kane. By the sound of his, he had no idea I got stuck in Sydney. I replied and told him to tell Nash and Matt I was okay before they texted me too.

I just pressed send when Dyson responded that he was all right, but missing me.

Blake sent a similar text a minute after that.

"When I said it was complicated..." I replied to Dyson and Blake and sat the phone on the table.

"You mean they all blow up your phone?" Leo finished.

"Not usually, no." We were often together, so there was no need for texting. When we weren't, the guys knew I might be alone with one of them and respected our space. I hadn't been apart from all of them and Ariana, or my parents, except when I was held in the lab. If it wasn't for Leo I would be very much alone. I didn't find the idea as appealing as I once might.

"Peyton," Leo said. I got the impression he'd said it a couple of times.

"Hmmm? Oh, sorry."

Johan stood beside the table, a plate on either hand. I leaned back so he could place mine in front of me. If it tasted half as good as it smelled, it would be wonderful.

"Thank you." I gave Johan a warm smile.

He grunted and moved away.

We can't charm everyone, I suppose.

"Eat up." Leo was already halfway through his first slice before I picked up mine and bit into it.

"Mmmm." It really was that good, even without the banana. I would have to bring all of the guys here sometime. And Ariana. They would all love this place. Well, maybe not the atmosphere. Gregor was still glaring as Leo over his glass of beer.

"What did I tell you, darlin'?" Leo asked.

"You were right?" I said with a mouthful of food.

"'Course I was. I usually am." He wiggled his eyebrows.

"There goes that modesty again."

"Maybe now you'll trust me." He gave me a speculative look and picked up another slice.

"You can lead a girl to pizza—"

"And her heart is yours forever?" he suggested. "It's an old saying."

"Old as in several seconds?" I asked.

He chuckled. "Something like that."

I smiled and plucked up the courage—maybe the wine helped—to ask another question.

"When do you use your demon face?"

"Oh, this?" He sat still for a moment as his skin turned red and rough-looking. Any sign of his tattoos disappeared. His head was completely free of hair of any kind. Even his eyebrows were gone. "Pretty, ain't I?"

That wasn't exactly the word I would have used, but I found him fascinating. Before I could stop myself, I reached out to touch his cheek. His skin was warm, but not as rough as it looked.

He caught my hand with his and raised it to his lips. The kiss he placed was soft, gentle.

"See, I'm not a big, scary demon. I'm a big softy, but don't go tellin' anyone."

"I didn't think you were scary," I said.

He looked a little disappointed for a moment.

"Not even a tiny bit?" he asked.

"Okay, maybe a teeny bit," I assured him.

"To answer your question, I only use this form to remind people of what I am, and when I'm with my mum. She says we shouldn't forget who we are and where we came from and all that." He let my hand go and shifted back to human form. "She says we shouldn't be ashamed. We're just shifters with a twist."

I smiled. "I like that. Shifters with a twist." I picked up my wine and sipped while trying not to look as though my hand was burning where he'd kissed it. Some people might have run when they saw his demon form, but I wanted him as much as I ever had.

He tilted his head. "Does anything scare you, darlin'?"

I snorted. "Lots of things. Zeta. Failing my classes. Losing people I care about."

He nodded. "Crickets on pizza?"

I laughed. "That's more yucky than scary." I regarded him for a moment. "Don't tell me, you like them?"

He shrugged. "They're an acquired taste. Like me."

"From what you've told me, I should probably run away and never look back."

"And yet, you're still here."

"Yes, I am," I agreed.

"And you're finished eating."

"As are you."

Leo waved toward Johan and handed him a couple of notes before he stood.

"There are rooms upstairs." Leo pointed toward one of the walls which loomed over us.

"Right, sounds good." My heart was pounding like a drum at a rock concert. I picked up my bag. "Lead the way."

"Whatever the lady desires." He took my bag and then my hand.

I didn't look back over my shoulder, but I sensed every eye in the restaurant was on us. They probably thought I was crazy and maybe I was, but I did trust Leo as much as I trusted any of my guys. *My guys? Since when had he become one of them?* That didn't matter so much as the fact he was.

The door clanged shut behind us and we headed toward a set of stairs. We had barely reached the landing outside the door to room three when Leo dropped the bags and pulled me into his arms.

Breathless, I let him draw me toward him. Our lips met in a burst of heat. He turned me and pressed my back to the door. His hands slid up my shirt and cupped my breasts. He ran a thumb over my nipple, making it instantly hard and sending a rush of warmth all through my body.

Before I was even aware of what he was doing, he'd tugged off my shirt and tossed it in the direction of our bags. Without any hesitation, he pulled down the cup of my bra and leaned down to close his mouth over my nipple.

"Maybe we should go inside," I suggested. Not because I was modest in the least anymore, but he might be getting carried away.

"I can't wait that long," he said around my nipple. He worked the button of my jeans loose and they joined my shirt on the ground. My panties followed.

"Foreplay next time," he promised. He unzipped his jeans and released his erection.

My eyes widened. He was bigger than I expected, but I ached to have him inside me. I didn't have to wait long. He hooked at am under my leg to lift it, pressed me against the door and slid himself into me.

"Oh gods," I moaned. He fit so tight it hurt at first. Gradually, my muscles relaxed to accommodate his thickness. Once they had, all I felt was good. Every fibre of me burned to feel his touch, inside and out.

He slid halfway out, then back in again. His cock massaged my insides, driving me closer to the edge already.

"You feel incredible, darlin'," he said breathlessly.

"So do you."

One more thrust and I came with a cry. I arched my back and let the fire consume me, burning through my veins and making me writhe against him to hold on just for a little longer.

He let out a hard grunt and came as well with a series of frantic thrusts. The moment I felt his hot cum flood inside me, something changed.

11

"So you and Dyson haven't had sex. Or…"

"Or what?" I pulled the blanket tighter around my shoulders and watched Leo over my glass of wine.

"Or you're not fated."

What the fuck?

"What the fuck?"

"Fated," he said again.

"You can say that all day, but that doesn't change the fact I have no idea what you're talking about." That was a lie, but not a flat out one. I understood it a little bit, just enough to freak me out.

"Is that something to do with whatever you did to me?"

He smiled and leaned over to refill my glass. He sat naked on the bed, apparently not worried in the slightest. Maybe that should have given me comfort, but it didn't.

"I didn't do anything to you, as such. It's a demon thing. Well, demons and dogs anyway."

"Like marking your territory?"

He grinned, but I sensed his desire to laugh. He suppressed it.

"How are you doing that?" I drank a gulp of wine bigger than I should have. Under the circumstances it was warranted.

"It's just part of the bond," he explained reasonably. "I suspected it was you, but I'm still as surprised as you are. Almost."

"I don't know if I need more wine or less for you to start making sense," I said dryly. "We had sex and now I feel your emotions. Can you feel mine?"

"Of course. Don't worry so much, darlin'. The bond won't hurt you. Quite the opposite."

"We'll see," I said darkly. "Did you do this on purpose?"

He threw back his head and laughed. "Nah. A demon can only bond with the person or people they're fated to be with. If they're lucky enough to find that person, a link is formed. It's a kind of magic, but it's older than... Well, just about everything."

"Can it be broken?"

He arched an eyebrow. "You wound me, darlin'. You don't want to sense my innermost feelings?" When I didn't answer, he added, "No, it can't be broken, but it can be minimised with distance."

"So we're meant to be together or something," I said uneasily. "What about the other guys?"

"You can bond with someone else, if they're a demon or a dog of some kind," Leo replied. "It's especially strong for wolves. I guess it's a wolf pack thing." He shrugged.

"But only if it's fated?" I ran a hand over my hair.

"Exactly. Hence my question about Dyson."

I licked my lips. "Would we have bonded if he…"

"Came down your throat?" Leo asked. "No, only if he was deep inside your warm, luscious—"

I held up a hand. "I see." I wasn't sure I did, but it made some kind of sense. I was drawn to Leo from the moment I'd seen him. If magic decreed we were supposed to be together, who was I to argue? The other guys might not be pleased though. I hated to think how Dyson would feel if we didn't form a bond. Part of me itched to track him down and find out. The other half was terrified of what might happen.

Or not happen.

"You can bond more than one person, too?" I asked finally.

"In theory, but one at a time." He smiled and took the glass from my hand. "I'm sorry if I scared you."

I looked at him from under my brows. "A little warning would have been nice, but if you weren't sure anything would happen, I'm not sure it would have helped."

"Would you have fucked me if I told you?" He grabbed the corner of the blanket and started to tease it away from my skin.

"Maybe not so soon," I said thoughtfully. "Although you are pretty irresistible."

"That's true." He kissed my cheek, then tickled my neck with his tongue. "I promised you foreplay, too."

"That's true, you did," I agreed. We had a lot more to talk about, but truthfully I needed to process this first. As strange things went, it was reasonably high on my list of things which happened to me recently. As far as I could tell, the bond was harmless, as long as Leo was. I liked to think I was a good judge of character, especially when choosing who to sleep with.

I put those thoughts aside for now. I would make more sense of it all later.

I hoped.

"Nice and slow then, hmmm?" He drew the blanket away from one breast, but left the rest of me covered.

"I like the sound of that."

He pressed me back against the mattress and let his tongue trail down over my chest. With featherlight touch, he licked the very tip of my nipple. Slowly, slowly, he traced circles around my sensitive peak, only touching it now and again.

"You're going to drive me crazy," I said breathlessly.

"That's the idea," he said, his voice muffled by his tongue. He pulled back and tugged the blanket back over my breast. Before I could object, he opened the other side and started to give the same teasing treatment to my other nipple.

As turned on as I got being exposed, there was something strangely arousing at having the layers peeled back only a little. It felt more intimate somehow, like he was focusing all of his attention on one part of me. At the same time, I felt his own arousal through the strange bond we had formed.

He closed the blanket over both breasts and moved down my body. He looked up and gave me a smile before he pulled the blanket back from my legs. He hooked one arm under my knee and bent it just enough to open me up to him.

He kissed his way up one thigh, then the other, before he tickled my sex with the tip of his tongue.

I shivered with the delicious warmth which coursed through me. From the bond I felt his appreciation for what he saw in front of him. It was a strange way to see myself, but I liked it.

He dove in a little further, licking and caressing me with practiced ease. His tongue darted around and over my clit. His eyes watched me, but I sensed he was using the bond to discern what I enjoyed. I wasn't sure if that was clever or cheating, but in the end I decided to stop thinking too much.

I closed my eyes and arched my back as he slid a finger into me. Then another.

"Gods," I murmured.

He lifted his head up just enough to smile before he lowered it and went back to licking at my clit and rubbing me from the inside with increasing rhythm.

I crested and tumbled over the edge in a wave that wasn't just mine. I felt his delight in hearing me cry out and buck against his hand and mouth. That heightened my orgasm to a place I had never been before. Blood pounded all through me so hard and hot I couldn't hear or feel anything but pleasure.

After a long plateau, I finally came down and flopped back against the mattress.

Leo emerged from between my legs and tugged the blanket off the rest of me. He rolled me onto my stomach and straddled my legs. Before I had even caught my breath, he gently pried my legs apart and slid his cock deep inside me.

He leaned down to whisper in my ear. "Gods, you are beautiful, inside and out." He cupped his hands over mine and started to move slowly inside me.

I felt how warm my insides were around his cock, how soft around his hardness. No wonder men liked sex so much, I felt amazing.

He pulled out and slid back in over and over, his breath becoming more and more ragged. The closer he got to coming, the more aroused I became.

Our breaths and bodies were in near perfect synch by now. The bond drove us closer and close to falling over the edge together. I had never felt anything like it. I didn't want it to end.

"Gods," he said near my ear. "I had no idea…" He thrust harder and harder until with a grunt he came hard. The bond gave me no choice but to follow.

Our voices cried out in perfect harmony. Whether this was fate or some magical bond created by peculiar circumstances, I didn't care. In the moment it was the most incredible sensation I had ever had. I felt myself contract around his cock, felt me milking him, felt his cum squirt out into my body. I sensed his pleasure and his joy.

Of course, he never bonded before either. This was new to both of us. It was something we could look forward to exploring together. As long as he didn't start to read my mind. A girl has to have some secrets.

Still in unison, we came down from the wild high together. He flopped down onto me before he rolled aside and drew me into his arms.

"I guess that's why they call it fate," he said softly. "I would only want to share that with someone I care about."

"Yeah," I agreed softly. The ugly memory of Fitz popped into my brain.

"I sense you're having dark thoughts." Leo propped himself up on one elbow. "Are you regretting this already?"

I frowned at him. "No, nothing like that." I considered telling him, but that would spoil this lovely, intimate moment. "Just ghosts from the past."

"Ah." He lay back down. "We all have those, darlin'."

I snorted softly. "You certainly seem to have a

few. I hope you're not going to drag me into any trouble?"

He chuckled. "Of course I am, but you'll love every minute of it."

"Oh? You think so huh?"

"I have no doubt whatsoever. Have I led you astray yet?"

I considered that for a moment. Unless he really had known about the bond, then he hadn't really. It wasn't his fault we missed the train, or that I had been drawn to him in the first place.

"No, but there's plenty of time for that to happen," I said finally.

He nuzzled my neck. "Yes there is and I can't wait for a moment of it. You and me, darlin' and all your other guys, we're in for one hells of a ride."

Honestly, that was what I was afraid of.

1 2

DYSON AND BLAKE were waiting for us at the train station in Illusion Bay when we arrived. The anxious expression on both of their faces could have been due to worry about me and Leo. It might also have been because of Nash, who stood a few metres away from them, his arms crossed over his chest. His face looked calm, but his eyes snapped with fire.

I couldn't tell if that anger was directed at me, or if he was pissed at himself for letting me out of his sight.

"Hey guys." I stepped off the train into humid air and a rush of embraces from Dyson, Kane, and even Matt.

"Trust you to get lost," Matt told me, a sideways smirk on his face.

I stuck out my tongue. "I love you, too." I might have been sarcastic, maybe not. Either way, he looked pleased.

Nash cleared his throat and everyone stepped back, leaving me to face him. After a moment he took my hand and led me off the platform toward a waiting van. It looked like something Scooby Doo would ride around in.

"Why in the name of the gods didn't you call me to come and get you?" he asked, his voice low. "You could have been—"

"I wasn't," I replied firmly. I appreciated his concern, but I was a grown woman, more or less capable of looking after myself. After all, I could shift into a nasty, bloodthirsty creature just like he could.

"I was perfectly safe the entire time. I don't need to be babied." I shook off his hand and narrowed my eyes at him.

His body stiffened. "I'm not trying to baby you. I care about your safety. Evidently more than you do."

I blinked at him a couple of times. "If I didn't care, I would have stayed in the lab and let them rape me," I snapped. "I have no intention of letting Zeta touch a hair on my head for as long as I live. If you think I would, you better think again, buddy."

I stuck out my chin and fixed my gaze on his face.

He seemed conflicted. On one hand, he knew I could be a badass, killing hybrid. On the other, I didn't want to be anything more than an ordinary witch, just conjuring up fluffy bunnies for shits and giggles. I didn't ask for any of this.

Finally, he exhaled. "I know. I'm sorry. I didn't mean to be a dick. It's just…"

"I know, you care, but leave being a dick to Matt," I said, half teasing.

"I heard that," Matt said from the other side of the van.

I chuckled. "Sorry, not sorry."

Nash took my hand and drew me to him. He nuzzled his face into the hair around my right ear. "I should tie you up and spank you for not calling me sir."

A delicious shiver traveled through my body and made my toes curl.

"Why don't you then, sir?"

"Maybe I will, after…" He trailed off and leaned back to look at me, a puzzled expression on his face. "What…" He glanced toward Leo and back.

"Fated mates, mate." Leo grinned.

"You can feel that?" I asked Nash.

"Yes, no…" Nash frowned. "I can feel something. It's like a strand of magic, like a bubble, but…not."

"Well that's as clear as mud," Kane said. He climbed into the front passenger seat and now sat staring at me.

I started to speak, but shook my head. "Maybe we shouldn't talk about this here."

"Yes," Nash replied immediately. "Let's get to the academy. It's an hour's drive from here as it is." He nodded to Matt who slipped into the driver's seat and started the van. It purred like a cat on steroids and smelled faintly like stale weed.

"Where did you find this thing?" I climbed in and sat between Nash and Blake. Blake changed into brightly coloured board shorts and a rumpled grey t-shirt. His curly hair was damp and the dimple in his cheek when he smiled was as cute as ever.

I returned his smile and placed a hand on his thigh, and one on Nash's when he sat beside me.

"It belongs to the college," Matt said over his shoulder.

"Do they use it to solve crimes?" I joked.

"They could now," Dyson said from the seat behind me. "We have a big, goofy dog."

"Awww," I twisted around and looked back at him. "You're not goofy." My gaze went to his lap and wondered if we could form a bond, too. Or he and Leo. They seemed to have taken to each other as well, judging by the looks they exchanged when the demon flopped down beside Dyson and stretched out like he was on a couch, not the back of a van.

"So, about that magic connection," Nash began.

"Right." I sat back around and explained what Leo had told me. Thankfully no one seemed bothered by my having slept with Leo in the first place. Blake and Dyson probably saw it coming—pun intended—as much as I had.

"Ain't never heard of anyone being able to sense a bond before, mate," Leo remarked, his accent thicker as he addressed Nash.

Nash shrugged. "I'm special."

I wasn't sure if he was joking or not, so I raised an eyebrow at him.

"Maybe it's because I'm a dragon," he said slowly. "Or it might be a hybrid thing."

"I can't sense anything," Matt said, "but my brain might be foggy from the second hand weed smoke in this godsdamned van."

I snorted softly. The longer I was in it, the stronger the smell became. "It doesn't run on weed fumes, does it?"

"It might," Kane said. "Technology is changing all

the time."

I giggled. "Oh goody, we could all have weed mobiles in a year or two."

"Who needs flying cars when you can get high like this?" Blake asked.

I giggled again.

Nash opened the window beside him to let in some fresh air.

I took the opportunity to peer out at the landscape as we rushed past. Through the trees I caught glimpses of the ocean and the occasional beach. Buildings of any kind were few and far between. Sub-tropical vegetation dominated the view instead.

"Are you sure there's a college up here?" I asked. "Please tell me there's no uniform."

"I hear on some days, clothing is optional," Dyson replied.

"I'm pretty sure that was an exaggeration," Kane said dryly.

"Why is nudity such a problem for you?" Dyson asked him. "You like having sex in public."

"I don't have a problem with nudity," Kane insisted. "Just yours. You're my brother, I don't want to see your dick."

"I do," Leo said.

"Me too," I agreed. "Dyson has a very nice dick."

"Oh, he does?" Leo asked, sounding very interested.

"Well, I don't want to brag," Dyson said.

Leo leaned forward so his breath brushed my neck. "Is it as nice as mine?"

I considered that for a moment. "I think it best if I don't answer that. I don't want to be seen to favour one dick over another."

"That's fair," Blake replied, "but you shouldn't decide until you've seen mine anyway."

"Oh, is that a promise?" My heart pounded.

He gave me a dimpled grin. "If you want it to be."

"Oh, I definitely do, but I'm still not going to favour one of you over the other."

"Does that mean you won't choose between us?" Kane asked.

The humid air in the van was suddenly hotter, but the guys all fell silent as though each held his breath.

"I..." I chewed my lip for a moment. "I don't want to choose. I care about you all equally. I want all of you. If that's a problem..."

"Not for me," Kane replied almost immediately.

"Me either," Dyson said.

"Or me, darlin'. You're stuck with me."

"And me as well," Nash said softly.

"There are worse clowns to be stuck with," Matt said from the driver's seat.

"Thanks, I think," I said dryly. I glanced over to Blake who was looking down toward his lap.

Without raising his head, he said, "I decided to go back to school so I could be around you. Whatever form that takes. I just hope you can find some time for me."

I put a hand on his arm. "Count on that. I'm looking forward to it."

He turned his head to the side and smiled. "Me too." His mouth worked before he was able to form more words. "Do you think we can make the same kind of bond you have with Leo?"

"Unless you're a dog or a demon, old boy—" Leo started.

"It's possible," Nash interrupted. "If you can form one with Dyson, I might be able to feel how it's done." He swung his head back toward Dyson. "Assuming you two plan to have sex and don't mind me listening in."

"You can watch us any time," Kane said helpfully.

"Noted," Nash replied. "Your twin isn't you. He

may prefer privacy. Although as I recall, that one time—"

"Yeah." Dyson's face was pink. "I suppose if we can form a bond, it's not fair if the rest can't. I mean, at least you could try to form one. If that means you have to… Yeah, I guess it would be okay."

"Good." Nash nodded. "I'm sure we can set up something suitably romantic."

"That would be nice," I said. "Because for a minute there I was feeling like a science experiment. I think we've established that I don't want to be in a lab."

Now Nash flushed. "It has to be all right with you as well. If we could bond, I would know…"

"You could keep a closer eye on me, sir?" I asked.

He hesitated. "That would be a benefit, yes."

"It would go both ways," I reminded him. "I would know if you're angry."

"You can't tell now?" he asked. "I need to work on that."

I chuckled. "You'd know how it feels to be spanked."

Rather than be put off by that, he seemed to find the idea appealing.

"Matt, can you drive a little faster?" Nash asked.

"Not without breaking the law now," Matt replied. "We're almost there anyway."

We swung into a narrow road which wound through trees covered in brightly coloured flowers. After a few minutes more, we came out into an open space with a beach on one side and a series of long, low buildings on the other.

"This is the college?" I asked in amazement.

"Yes." Matt said over his shoulder. "Welcome to the College of Advanced Magical Education. C. A. M. E."

I snickered at the acronym, but I preferred this to the original AMM campus or the one which belonged to the UA. Compared to those, this looked warm, relaxed, and inviting, rather like a resort. All it needed was a few hammocks here and there and a cocktail bar. Although, for all I knew, those might be around here somewhere.

"Please tell me we're not in the basement, or sleeping on the beach?" I climbed out behind Nash and reached for my bag.

"Oh no, nothing like that," Dyson assured me. "Come on, you'll love it." He took my hand and sent a jolt of heat through me.

At that moment, I wasn't sure if I could be happier, sounded by a bunch of guys I adored, in the warm air beside the beach and anticipating the night to come. What more could a hybrid want?

Okay, in the back of my mind I was worried whether we'd be accepted at this campus and if Zeta would find us here. I just wanted to finish my education in peace.

Was that too much to ask?

13

"You don't have to do this you know." Dyson's face was distorted by my champagne glass. Bubbles rose in front of him, slowly sliding upward to burst at the top.

I took a sip and set the glass aside.

He grimaced. "It's not that I don't want to. It's just..." He jerked his thumb toward the curtain which covered the open window. Every so often a breeze would ruffle it and blow it inward a fraction.

Nash and Matt sat outside, ready to see if either could sense anything which might indicate a bond forming. Nash seemed sure he'd know if it worked. Matt—he seemed more curious than anything, but sceptical as well. I suspected he wouldn't believe bonds existed until he felt one for himself. Fair enough, I wouldn't have believed it if Leo had merely told me about it.

I crossed my legs. "They're probably on their phones," I remarked. "Would you feel better if they were in the room?"

"Gods, no," Dyson said immediately. "Any other time I might, but not now." He cupped my cheek gently. "I want this to be about you and me. Well, as much as it can be."

"I could tell them to get lost." I uncrossed my ankles and placed my hand on the bed, ready to push myself to my feet if necessary.

Dyson caught my hand. "I'd never hear the end of it from Kane. He wants to bond with you too. If there's a chance, he would take it with both hands. I'd bet anything Nash, Matt, and Blake feel the same way."

I arched an eyebrow at the direction of the window, but if either guy heard, they didn't respond. At least, not that I could hear. For all I knew, they were using sign language to have an intense discussion on the best cop movie ever made and not paying us any attention.

What? Cop movies are okay.

"That doesn't mean you're obligated in any way," I said firmly. "They'll deal with it." They were all big boys after all, more than capable of handling all sorts of things, including this.

Dyson shrugged. "After tonight, I'm taking you somewhere private so we can take our time with no interruptions."

As if on cue, Leo's voice came in through the window.

"Is this where you ole boys got to?" he asked easily.

Nash replied but his words were muffled.

"Oh, don't mind if I join you then? I love a little voyeurism. Move over then, lads."

"We're not here to watch." Nash sounded annoyed. "We're just observing the bond, if there is one. This all might be for nothing."

"Bet you ten bucks it won't be," Leo replied.

"Ten bucks? What do you know that we don't?" Matt asked.

"A shit ton, probably," Leo said with a laugh. "Seriously though, it's obvious."

"You think?" Nash asked. "If you could tell us how the bond is formed, we could leave them to it."

"No can do, big guy," Leo said. "I don't know either. I just know they have a connection." After a pause, he added, "Don't dragons have dog DNA? That's why you're here, isn't it? Your ego can't stand the fact you don't have a bond. If you're not meant to be, you're not—"

Nash cut him off. "I don't believe this bond is some kind of godsmade gift. It's just a kind of magic and most magic can be reproduced in some way."

"I guess we'll find out, eh?" Leo said.

"Only if you shut up," Matt snapped.

Dyson sighed softly and leaned back against the pillows. "Now I know how lab rats feel."

I snorted. "Maybe we both need more champagne. Or we could sneak out the door and hide somewhere?"

He grinned. "I'm surprised Kane didn't insist on being my fluffer."

I slapped a hand over my mouth to stifle a loud laugh. After a moment or two, I lowered it and said, "That would take awkward to a whole new level. Although, I could ask Leo in to do it if you like."

Dyson chuckled and reached for me. "I have a better idea. How about we forget all about them and focus on each other."

"That's the best idea I've heard all day." I leaned in to claim his mouth with mine. The kiss we shared was searing hot and left me breathless. We kissed before, but never like this.

"Wow," I said against his mouth.

"Mmmhmm," he agreed. "You set me on fire."

"Not literally, I hope." Phoenixes and fire went hand in hand, or was that hand in wing? At least in mythology they did. In real life, I didn't breathe flames, or get reborn from any ashes.

Yet.

Give it time, I was probably not done with the weirdness. Or it wasn't done with me.

He chuckled again. "No, but my insides are burning up." He reached for the hem of my shirt and tugged it up and over my head. He tossed it aside and unhooked my bra after a few tries.

"I've never done that before," he admitted as he cupped my breast and ran a thumb over my nipple. "I've thought about this a thousand times."

"Only a thousand?" I teased.

"At least that."

I helped him out of his shirt and ran my fingertips down his abs. "What do you have under there, rock?"

"Just hard work," he assured me. "And pizza."

"Pizza makes for great abs?" I asked. Hells yeah. If that was the case, I would eat more of it.

"No, but it's a great reward for working out."

"I don't think that's how it's supposed to work." I

shuffled down a little and ran the tip of my tongue over his firm torso.

"No?" He tangled his fingers in my hair.

"Nuh-uh." I shook my head and undid the front of his shorts. I thought he might have been turned off by the guys outside the window, but his erection said otherwise. His cock was hard and hot in my hand. I licked his tip and tasted the bead of cum which had already formed there.

"You might want to save some of that." His voice was strained already.

"Good point." But I still sucked the head of his cock a few more times and massaged his balls with my fingers and nails.

When he groaned, I moved away and tossed my shorts onto the floor.

"Tease," he said jokingly.

"You'd better believe it." I grinned and lifted my hips as he pushed my panties off them and down my legs.

His eyes raked down my body, taking in every bit of me. "You're also the most beautiful woman I have ever seen. I'm the luckiest guy on the face of the planet right now."

I felt Leo's response through our bond. I thought he might joke around, but he agreed with Dyson and was turned on. That in turn heightened my own arousal. Bonding with all the guys might get interesting if I was turned on every time they were. I had a healthy enough sex drive as it was.

"You're going to make me blush."

"I'd prefer to make you scream." His mouth closed on my nipple. He drew it in between his lips and sucked like I was a delicious morsel.

"That could happen too." I arched my back, aroused as hells by his touch, but also knowing the guys were listening. In some ways, it was almost more enticing than having them watch. This way they would have to use their imaginations to visualise what might be going on inside. If theirs were anything like mine, it would be wild.

"There's something you should know," Dyson said around a mouthful of nipple. He swapped to the other, leaving the first to glisten in the light of the candles the other guys had lit for us. "I've never done any of this before. With anyone."

He lifted his head and looked at me as though he was worried about how I'd react.

"I thought you might not," I said gently. "Or you might have bonded with them."

He cocked his head to the side. "That's true. You don't mind?"

I held his gaze with mine and hoped he saw my desire. "I'm honoured," I said firmly.

He smiled with relief. "I want you so bad."

"I want you too." Mostly because I just did, but part of me was dying to know if the bond would form or not. If it didn't, I wasn't sure who would be more disappointed, Dyson or me. Or Kane, who apparently has almost as much invested in this. I was surprised he wasn't sitting outside with the others. Then again, maybe he was and was just more quiet than they were.

The idea of him listening in made my skin tingle all over. My imagination threw Blake in as well, then they started to touch each other…

Dyson rolled me onto my back and lay between my spread knees. With most of his weight on his huge arms, he leaned in to cover my mouth with his.

I returned his kisses with all the heat which rushed through my veins. I opened my mouth and teased his lips.

I rolled us both until I straddled his hips. He looked up at me with such love, my heart reacted a little harder. I sensed he forgot about the guys outside. This was all about us now.

I positioned myself over his cock and slid down his cock. Tentative at first, then a little deeper.

He groaned. "I didn't know you'd feel so amazing." He closed his eyes, an expression of pure bliss on his face. "I mean, I suspected." He caressed my breasts lightly, thumbs brushing over my taut nipples.

I laughed softly. "Same to you."

Let's face it, not all cocks are created equal. They're all epic, but they feel different. Not different bad or necessarily different good, just different. And this one I was enjoying thoroughly, deep inside me.

"You think so?" He cracked open one eye and gave me a lopsided smile.

Of course Dyson would crack jokes during sex. It was another part of his charm.

"Absolutely. I've imagined this since I first saw your dick. This is next level amazing."

"Thank you, on behalf of my dick and I." He closed his eyes as I rose and fell, riding him slowly.

"You're welcome." I closed my own eyes and let my arousal and Leo's carry me closer to the edge of the abyss. I wanted to tumble over, but not yet. First, I wanted to savour the first time between Dyson and I. It had been a long time coming.

Pun intended.

"Peyton," Dyson whispered.

"Yes?"

"I love you."

"I love you, too."

He rolled us over again and pulled out of me and rolled me onto my side.

"I want to be able to see your face better." He gently guided one of my legs over his and opened me up to him. One hand cupped my cheek, the other guided him back into me.

We lay there like that for what seemed like an eternity, eyes locked on each other, his thrusts slow but rhythmic. My passion simmered, coming closer and closer to the boil.

After a long while, he increased his speed. He reached in between us to gently caress my clit.

"Come for me," he whispered.

I drew my lower lip in between my teeth and bit gently. I wanted, needed to come, but I didn't ever want this to end.

He rubbed a little harder, always at the right angle, in exactly the right place. Maybe we had formed a bond already; he was that in-sync with my body. Maybe he just knew where to find a clit.

I puffed a breath out my nose, then another.

The pressure built until I couldn't contain it any longer. I threw back my head and cried out, long and low as my orgasm rocked my from the top of my head to the tips of my curled toes.

"Ohhh, Dyson," I breathed.

"Peyton…" He thrust harder still and grunted.

My eyes snapped open the moment he came.

I felt his body tense.

His cock, hard and deep inside me squirted cum like a fountain of heat and magic. It flooded into me, through me. It traveled from my belly through every drop of my blood, every organ, right up into my heart, my mind.

It was different to the one Leo and I had formed, but it was undeniable.

We were bonded.

The profound silence was broken by Leo's shout of triumph. "You blokes owe me ten bucks!"

14

"SO, DID YOU FEEL ANYTHING?" I pulled out a chair and flopped down beside Nash. I stifled a yawn and stole a slice of Vegemite toast from his plate. After Leo's shout, the guys had left Dyson and I to enjoy the rest of the night in peace. And enjoy it we did, twice more. When I crept out of bed, he was still snoring.

I smiled at Kane who had been scrolling madly through his phone, but now put it aside.

"Yeah." Nash scowled as I bit into the toast. "I felt the bond form. I was right, it is just magic."

"It sounds to me like the release of a pheromone," Kane said. "In animals, they help to attract a mate. In humans, too. Basically it…influences the behaviour of the other person, or people."

He gave me a lopsided grin that looked so much like his twin, my heart skipped. I adored both of them so much. I couldn't imagine my life without them.

"So this magic pheromone created a bond?" I asked.

"Pheromones can work to synchronise two creatures, so basically, yes." Kane nodded.

I considered for a moment. "Was it something I did last night that did it? A conjuring I didn't know existed until Leo?" I scratched behind my ear. "That doesn't explain how he and I formed a bond too, though. He can't do magic, can he?"

"He's a shifter, more or less," Nash pointed out. "That in itself is magic."

I nodded slowly. "Of course it is."

"Bond-forming and shifting might be his only magic. Dyson's too, evidently." Kane grimaced slightly.

I leaned over to cover my hand with his. "What you do with your tongue is magic."

He flushed bright red and mumbled his thanks.

"You didn't consciously do magic?" Nash asked, interrupting the awkward moment.

"No, I just...enjoyed myself," I replied. "Why? Did it feel as if I did?"

Nash picked up his mug of coffee and held it without drinking for a few moments. "Not that I could tell, but all I know is magic flashed between you two and the bond was there."

"Magic cum," I mused.

"That or you have a magic pussy," Kane said.

"She certainly has that," Nash agreed.

Now I blushed. "Maybe it needs both."

Nash frowned. "That's something we could try."

I raised both eyebrows at him as high as they'd go. "Are you planning to use Dyson's cum to create a bond?"

His mouth dropped open in surprise. "I wasn't, but now you mention it—"

"I suspect it will only work once," Kane said. "It's caused its chemical—or magical—reaction. It might work with someone else, but not with Peyton again."

"What will then?" Nash asked. "Regular magic?"

Kane rubbed his chin. "It might, but I feel as though if it was that simple, everyone would be doing it."

Both guys let out simultaneous heavy sighs.

"It can't hurt to try though, right?" I finished my toast and washed it down with a sip of water from Kane's glass. I needed tea, but it would have to wait.

Before Kane could move, Nash put aside his coffee and took my hand in his. He closed his eyes.

I sensed him drawing magic from all around us. "What now?" I whispered, not wanting to break his concentration entirely.

He shook his head. "I don't know. I'm thinking about the bond, but I don't feel anything forming."

"Neither do I." I drew a little too, and delved around for where his magic met mine. We could have formed a large bubble, or knocked everyone in the room off their feet. There was no sign of a bond.

After a while I exhaled and let the magic go.

Nash did the same. "Either it has to involve sex, or there's more to it than that. As much as I'd love to find out if it's the first one, I have to get to work. You have classes too, no doubt."

"Ugh, the real world." I groaned to add a little extra melodrama to the moment.

Kane chuckled. "I'm looking forward to it. I hear the facilities here are nice and warm."

"Thank the gods." After the rooms at UA, I was ready for a nice, humid lecture theatre or whatever they had here.

"Just try not to piss anyone off," Nash warned.

"Who, me?" I pointed at myself. "I never *try* to

annoy anyone, it just happens." I smiled as innocently as I could.

He snorted. "Just don't mention Zeta or anything about them coming after you and you should be fine."

"I was trying to avoid even thinking of them," I said. Nash was right though. The antagonism between me and some of the students at UA was less about me and more about their fear Zeta would come after them. The joke would be on them though, if they knew Zeta *owned* the University of Arcana. Still, I wouldn't even wish life in a lab on Xav, the guy who had been the biggest dick in UA.

"Don't get complacent either," Nash added. "The council assures me you're safe here, but don't turn your back on anyone. Just in case."

"Yes, sir," I said smartly. I even threw in a salute for good measure.

His eyes shone and I knew he was rethinking having to work. I suspected he'd prefer to tie me down to his bed and spank my ass until it was red.

He placed his hands on the table and pushed himself to his feet. The bulge in his pants confirmed my suspicions.

"I will see you later," he said, his voice heavy. He nodded to Kane and hurried away.

I watched his tight ass until he was obscured from view, and turned to Kane.

"I'm sorry."

He looked surprised. "What for?"

"Because your brother and I bonded, but we haven't. It's not for lack of trying."

"Maybe if we'd known we could, we would have done something differently," he said.

"Your parents never mentioned a bond?"

"No, never."

"Are they dog shifters?"

"No. Dad is a big cat. Our mother is a bird. They think the wolfhound came from our dad's mother."

I ran a hand over my hair. "So shifters can be quite different, even within families. Are any of you part demon?"

Kane considered for a moment. "It's possible. Maybe dogs and demons share more characteristics in common."

"I've never heard of demons humping people's legs," I said with a smile.

Kane choked back a laugh. "Me either, but Leo looks like the kind who would."

"What would I do, big guy?" Leo appeared behind us and slid into the chair Nash vacated. "Oh look, you left me a half drunk cup of cold coffee."

"Feel free." I waved toward the mug.

"I'll pass. I prefer it fresh and hot, just like you, darlin'" He pressed a kiss to my mouth.

Kane cleared his throat.

"Oh, sorry." Leo turned and planted a sound kiss on Kane's mouth which ignited my blood faster than a match.

Kane blushed bright red, but didn't look as though he minded.

Oh gods, now them being together would be in my carousel of fantasies.

"We should be getting to class," I said regretfully.

"Bah, there's plenty of time for class." Leo waved his hand in a gesture of dismissal. "Wouldn't you prefer to sneak out and explore Illusion Bay? Just the two of us. Okay, three of us." He winked at Kane.

"I don't mean to be rude," Kane said, "but why are you here? Apart from your bond with Peyton, I mean."

Leo rubbed his forehead with his fingertips. For a few moments he actually looked serious.

"I'm trying to find my place in the world. I know it involves Peyton and you guys, but apart from that..." He shrugged and the smile returned to his face. He sat back and crossed his arms over his chest.

"Maybe I'll get a job. Or I might find the local nudist beach and get a tan."

"Don't get a sunburnt cock," I advised him. "That might hurt."

Kane winced. "Yeah, it does. I mean, it would. I wouldn't know." His face was red again and he looked away.

"I'll bet there's a story there, old boy," Leo said lightly, "but it'll have to wait. We have a town to discover." He held out his hand to me.

"I really can't," I replied after a few moment's thought. "It's our first day of classes and they've been nice enough to let us study here."

Leo huffed. "Responsible adult, hmmm?"

"What can I say?" I shrugged. "One of us has to be."

"I thought that was Nash's job?"

"It is, but he's not here right now, so I have to step up." A smile tugged at the corners of my mouth.

Leo grimaced playfully. "I hope it's not contagious."

"It probably is. Why, are you regretting bonding with me now?"

"Not for a moment, but I should go before I turn into my father."

"Well we wouldn't want that." I nodded.

Leo's nose wrinkled. "Gods no. He's an accountant. So is my older brother. And my younger one. I'm the only fun one in the whole family."

Kane patted his hand. "That must be a terrible burden."

Leo sighed dramatically. "It really is. Family events are so dull."

"I never would have thought of demons as boring," I said.

"Until you saw me, you didn't know we existed," Leo pointed out. "Except on TV and in movies."

"I'm assuming those aren't accurate representations, just like witches and shifters?" I asked.

"Oh, I don't know. I know plenty of demons who..." Leo flinched and looked past my shoulder. "Shit."

"What?" I turned around in my seat and glanced back. I didn't see anything unusual, just a group of students gathered around talking. They all wore t-shirts or singlets and shorts; a refreshing change from the uniforms UA had made us wear.

"Them," Leo said. "They're all demons."

"Oh." I looked at them closely. They didn't look like anything out of the ordinary, certainly nothing to be afraid of.

"Which one did you piss off?" Kane asked.

"All of them," Leo replied.

I turned back around in time to see him stand and push his chair back under the table. Before he could step away, one of the other demons called his name.

"Leo! What the hells are you doing here?" A woman with long red hair and a nose ring walked toward him, hips swaying. She smiled, but her eyes snapped with barely contained annoyance.

"Cordelia." Leo spoke from between clenched teeth. "I thought I'd get an education. Wasn't that your suggestion?"

She smirked. "I believe my words were along the lines of, "if I ever see you again, I'll teach you a lesson." Are you dumb enough to come back for more?"

He raised his hands. "I guess so, love." He loudly whispered, "Cordelia is an old family friend. She likes to think she's queen of the demons. Maybe of all paranormals."

Cordelia snorted. "That's bullshit. I just don't put up with Leo and his crap." She held out a hand to me. "Welcome to the college. Don't believe a word Leo says." To my surprise, she gave me a wink.

I found myself shaking her hand and smiling at her. I had the feeling whatever there was between them was a lot of words, but mostly a friendly rivalry. I hope so. I'd had enough of aggressive students and assholes.

"You *must* come to the party tonight on the beach. We're inviting the entire college, especially you guys from AMM. I've heard whispers that you dealt with an attack from Zeta."

She was clearly fishing for information. Truthfully I didn't know how to reply to that.

I shrugged. "You shouldn't believe everything you hear."

She smiled. "I never do. That's why I want to hear it all first hand. But it can wait until tonight. You will come, right?"

I glanced back to see Kane nod.

Leo made a choking sound, but said, "We wouldn't miss it."

"There you are then," I said lightly. I might tell her a bit about the attack, but if I could, I would also ply her and her friends for information about the bond. This could work in both our favours.

15

THE MUSIC THROBBED HARDER than my heart. The slip and crunch of hot sand changed to a cool squelch under my feet as I reached the waterline. A wave washed up the beach and over my bare feet.

I squealed. "It's so cold!"

"As cold as Cordelia's heart," Leo said. He scowled down at his damp pant legs.

I reached for his arm and tugged him closer to me. "Are you going to be a killjoy all night?"

"If he is, you can ditch him and dance with me," Dyson said easily.

"Me first." Kane took hold of my hand and laced his fingers in mine.

"No way, I—"

I cut Dyson off. "Don't make me throw you both in the drink so you cool down."

"You wouldn't?" Dyson asked with mock horror.

"She might not, but I would," Matt said from behind them.

"I'd help Matt," Nash remarked.

I looked back and caught his eye. He looked good back in track pants and a singlet; comfortable and with more of his muscled body on display. I loved seeing him in a suit, but this was the Nash I knew and loved. I could have torn off his singlet and licked his abs then and there, but instead I gave him a smile full of promise.

"You would?" I asked teasingly.

He shrugged. The corner of his mouth turned up in a slight smile. "Whatever it takes to break up a fight." His expression darkened and I knew what he was thinking. As long he didn't have to kill, he'd take part.

"We'll be good," Kane said in a hurry. "But if you want us to take our clothes off, you only have to ask."

"Take your clothes off." Leo grinned.

Kane blushed, bright red. "Maybe later," he muttered.

"I'll hold you to that, big boy." Leo clapped him on the back. "Oh look, alcohol."

If there was anything that might change the subject, it was that. We all stopped chatting and gathered around a huge table to grab a cup and fill it with beer.

"Here you are." Blake handed me a cup before I could get one myself.

"Thanks." I took the cup and shot him a smile.

"Do you actually dance?" he asked.

I grimaced. "Not very well. I'm more the type to sway, more or less in time with the music. You?"

He looked embarrassed. "I used to do competitive ballroom dancing. It's been years since I've done it," he added quickly.

My eyes widened. "You must have been really good. Did you win a lot of the dance-offs, or whatever they're called?"

He chuckled. "A few. It was fun, except..."

"Except what?" I prompted.

"Except the mothers at the dance school used to go on about my curly hair." He sipped and made a face. "You'd think they'd never seen a guy with curls before." He ran a hand over his head absently.

"I like your curls," I assured him. Would it be wrong of me to admit that was the first thing I noticed about him? To be fair, he was pretending to be a loyal Zeta guard at the time. I was hardly going to be looking at his ass. I had done that a lot since.

He looked pleased, but smiled ruefully. "I like your hair better, especially the green streak." He tilted his head. "Is that a permanent colour? You've had it since I've known you and it doesn't seem to be growing out."

I touched my head lightly. "Magic gone awry," I said simply. "Courtesy of Ariana." A flood of emotion filled me. I missed her. Nash still hadn't explained where she'd gone and I didn't push. I knew he would only tell me when he was ready to. While that bugged the hells out of me, arguing with him would get me exactly nowhere.

"I could probably fix that if you want?" Blake offered.

"It's okay, I kind of like it now." I lowered my hand. "I want to hear more about your dancing. Or better yet, see it."

"On sand?" He glanced toward his feet. "It's not exactly the best dance floor."

"Why not?" I tapped my bare toes on the sand. "It's a little wet, I suppose."

"Just a little," he agreed. "Maybe later. Can we sway first?"

I glanced around to see the rest of the guys, beers

in hand, talking about some movie we streamed the night before. I fell asleep in the middle of it, but evidently they'd enjoyed it.

"Sure." I offered him my hand and we moved away to let others get to the drinks table.

Blake wound an arm around me and, careful not to spill our drinks, we swayed. His body pressed hard against mine and made my heart race faster than before.

"This is nice," he said near my ear. "It's hard to get you alone."

I snorted softly. "It's hard to be alone," I agreed. "Not that I'd change a thing," Truthfully, they gave me space when I really needed it, as long as it was safe enough. Which translated to not as often as I'd like, but hopefully being here would change things. I was desperate for something close to normal, maybe even boring, for a little while.

"Can I cut in?" a smooth voice asked.

"Uh." Blake stepped back before Cordelia all but shoved him out of the way. "I guess so."

I gave him a regretful look and mouthed, "Later," before Cordelia took my hand and wound an arm around me.

"If you haven't guessed before now, I like girls,"

she said bluntly. "I want you to know I want to kiss you, badly."

"I…" I swallowed. I wasn't sure how to respond to that. I couldn't say I hadn't kissed girls before, but not recently. Ariana and I were just friends and I wasn't close enough to anyone else to even think about it.

"It's okay if you don't feel the same way," she said lightly. "I just prefer to be honest."

"Right," I replied. "Of course. I appreciate that." I really did.

"There's no need to rush things." She twirled us around. "I'm sure you have lots of questions about demons. You want to know about the bond, right?"

While I stammered, she smiled. "I'm very astute. Besides, I know Leo. He wouldn't hang around long unless there was something in it. It's either a bond or he's running a scam." She cocked her head to the side so her hair fell over her shoulder. "I wouldn't rule out both, just between us. Keep an eye on that one."

"Right," I said slowly. "What kind of scam?" If she was trying to sew seeds of doubt, she succeeded.

She laughed, a tinkling sound which unnerved at the same time it drew me to her. "Oh the gods know with him. Gambling, blackmail… If it's illegal, he'll do it. It's funny how people like bad boys. And bad girls too, of course." She ran the tip of her tongue over her lips.

I swallowed hard. "Yeah, funny about that." I tried to clear my thoughts, but they were hazy, as if I had more than a few sips of beer. "So, you were going to tell me about the bond?" If I didn't know better, I'd think someone slipped something funny into my drink. Blake wouldn't do that and I held my drink myself ever since he handed it to me. Maybe it was just her.

"I could be persuaded to… Are you feeling okay? You look a little pale."

I blinked at her worried face, but she was a blur.

"Maybe you should sit down."

"Yeah." I took a step away, but staggered before she caught me.

"Wow, you must be a real lightweight." She laughed. "One drink and you're tripping over. Come on, I'll help you."

"I didn't…only had a sip." My speech was slurred, as if I'd downed a bottle of vodka and it just hit me.

"You what?" She wound her arm under mine and helped me off the side, out of the lights they set up for the party.

"I only had a bit." I tipped my cup and upended

the rest of my beer on the sand. When it hit, it sizzled slightly before it sank between the grains.

"Those fucking idiots," she growled.

"What?" I muttered. I leaned against her and closed my eyes. "Please don't tell me it's Zeta?"

"If it is, I'll tear their heads off with my bare hands. But no, it's not them."

"Hey Cordy." A new voice spoke, smooth, like honey laced with arsenic.

"Sawyer," she replied darkly. "What did you do to her?"

He laughed, deep and low. "Just having a little fun. You know how these witches are. They think they're better than us. It's time to take them down a peg or two."

"I'm not a witch," I mumbled. I felt the familiar sensation of anger burning at me. My inner phoenix itched to get out. Forget tearing heads off, I would rip the demon into ribbons so small his parents wouldn't be able to identify him.

Sawyer crouched down in front of me and crossed his arms. "You're a slut with more dicks than holes. I'm sure you're itching for one more." He grabbed his groin and sneered.

"Fuck off," I said as clearly as I could manage. I

tried to draw in magic and knock the asshole off his feet, but it wouldn't come.

"That's the idea. Come on guys, grab an arm each. You can have a go when I'm done."

"No way." Cordelia shot to her feet. "I'm not going to let you do this."

"Get out of the way Cordy. You said yourself she wanted to know about the bond. Who better to show her?"

"Not like this, Sawyer," she growled. "Do you think those guys won't come looking?"

Of course they will, I thought. Any minute now.

Sawyer laughed. "Do you think I'm stupid? They all drank the beer, too."

Fuck.

I reached out to Dyson and Leo through the bond, but found only Leo's befuddled thoughts. Dyson seemed to be out cold already.

A hot tear trickled down my cheek.

Fingers dug into my skin as Sawyer's friends hauled me to my feet. I tried to shrug them off, but my body wouldn't respond with more than a twitch.

Fuck.

"Can't you just tell me about the bond?" I asked, with what spirit I had left.

"Hells no, it's much more fun if we show you." Sawyer leered into my face.

"Sawyer," Cordelia said insistently.

"You can help, or you can get out of the way."

I turned heavy, but pleading eyes to her. *Yes, help. Help me!*

She stood for a few moments, wide eyed and horrified, just in the edge of the light. She let out a long breath, then stepped aside.

"Good girl." Sawyer nodded. "Bring that one, too." He waved toward a figure who lay slumped on the sand a few metres away. Kane.

What the hells? What kind of twisted game were they trying to play? The idea of them hurting Kane made my fury rise like throwing fuel on a fire. I gritted my teeth and tried to shift. To hells with being nice, I would tear them all to pieces and feast on their bones. I suck their veins dry of every drop of blood. I would coat my claws in their gore. If I found brains in their heads, I would eat those too, hot and raw with their last, terrified thoughts.

I gritted my teeth, but the shift wouldn't come. All it did was burn away the last of my energy. I blinked, but keeping my eyes open was almost impossible.

"Give in," Sawyer said in my ear. "Sleep. When you wake, we'll have some fun."

Fuck you. The words wouldn't come though. I slumped and was caught up in someone's arms. The last thing I knew, I was carried into the darkness.

The last thought I had before sleep claimed me was, N*ot again.*

16

"WAKEY WAKEY." A hand tapped my cheek.

I jerked away, but regretted it immediately. Partly because I had the headache from hells and partly because they knew I was awake and regained some use of my body. Had I waited, I could have shifted and torn them to shreds without them knowing I was coming.

"Come on." Fingers pinched my earlobe.

"Fuck off." I lashed out with a punch and connected with a hard thigh.

Sawyer chuckled. He rose and moved away. "The witch has some bite to her, huh?"

"You have no idea," I muttered. I opened my eyes and pushed myself up to sit in the sand. A fire crackled a few metres away. Sawyer's friends sat around it, drinking beer from bottles and passing around what looked like a joint.

"What the fuck?" I squinted at them, then down at myself. I didn't seem to have been interfered with in any way.

Yet.

"You want some?" A guy with blonde hair and what looked like scales on his cheeks offered me the joint.

"Um, no thanks, I'm good." I raised a hand slightly.

"Mmmm-kay." He put it to his lips and took a drag.

Sawyer flopped down in front of me and crossed his legs. "Sorry for the subterfuge, but we can't let any old person know about the bond."

I bared my teeth at him. "The last person who put me to sleep and abducted me died a horrible death. You have exactly three seconds to tell me why I shouldn't do the same to you."

He held out his hand and opened it. On his palm lay two stones, both red and shaped like a circle. Leather necklaces dangled between his fingers.

"Because I have bonding stones."

"So what?" I asked. "If you even try to touch me, I'll rip your throat out."

He chuckled. "Trust me, you're not my type. I prefer demons."

"Bigot." I kept one eye on him and the other on the stones.

He shrugged. "Once bitten, twice shy."

I snorted. "A witch bit you?" I was tempted to do the same. "Did you drug and threaten to assault her too."

He gave me a sideways smile. "Cordy tells me I have a sick sense of humour. The drugging was necessary, so you don't know where you are. We can't have people turning up here."

I frowned. "Where is here?" To me it looked like an ordinary section of beach.

"Why would I go to all this trouble only to tell you that?"

"You still haven't given me a reason why I shouldn't shift and rip your head off, then fly away," I said sweetly. "From the air I'd find out where I am pretty fast."

For a moment his bravado slipped. "I'm starting to think I shouldn't help you at all. Maybe I should have cut your throat while you slept."

"There's that sick sense of humour again," I said. I wasn't sure he was joking until he grinned.

"Yeah, I wouldn't want to mess my clothes with

witch blood. Or hybrid." He narrowed his eyes. "What are you?"

"I can't think of a single reason why I should tell you that." I sniffed. With any luck, the rest of the guys were waking up and looking for me. Although, I wasn't sure I really was in any trouble, as such. I mean, apart from the whole abduction thing.

I glanced to the side to see Kane start to twitch.

Sawyer shrugged. "So you want to know about bonding? Let me guess, you know magic is involved?"

"Do I?" I asked. When he didn't reply, I sighed. "Fine. Yes, we know that much. We also know it involves dogs and demons, or some combination of both."

"The bond originated with dog shifters. Some nosy witch managed to emulate it with magic."

I frowned at his continued bigotry, but said nothing.

He tossed the stones in his hand. "She shared the information with her demon lover. Between them, they started the story about fated mates and it went from there. That was over a hundred years ago now. The witch passed the secret to her daughters and to this day, only a handful know how to do it. The Demon Collective keeps a tight rein on them. If every witch knew, she'd have every man under her spell." He made a face as though he'd eaten something sour.

"You keep saying witches," I pointed out, my voice tight with annoyance at his attitude. "What about wizards?"

He hesitated. "As far as I know, it's only witches who can do it. The gods only know if any wizards have tried. I'm not privy to that information."

"So you don't know everything," I said dryly. "There's a shock."

He raised his eyebrows, but then grinned. "Not everything, just most things."

I turned my face as Kane groaned and rolled over, but didn't wake.

"He'll be fine," Sawyer said. "So do you want to try one?" He held up a bonding stone.

"I'm not bonding you." I curled my lip at him.

He snorted. "Thank the gods for that. These stones will allow us to feel the bond, but the moment we take them off, it'll be gone. Careful though, you'll bond any cock that comes inside you before the magic wears off."

"So we'd have to have sex to make the bond permanent?" I asked carefully.

"Yeah, that's what he's for." Sawyer jerked his chin

toward Kane. "You're not going to believe me until that happens."

"Why do you care if I believe you or not?" I asked.

"I don't, but Cordy will get the shits with me."

"Cordy likes girls," I pointed out.

"No shit," Sawyer snorted. "She's my sister."

"Oh."

He tossed me a stone and put the other around his neck.

"If this goes badly, I will kill you," I told him. I hadn't ruled out doing that anyway. The sweat from my fear hadn't dried on my skin yet.

I took a closer look at the stone. If I didn't know it was full of magic, I would have just thought it was a cheap trinket. Hells, it might be cheap anyway. It felt warm on my palm, as though it was alive somehow. That was a disconcerting thought.

"We're here for a good time, not a long time," Sawyer pointed out.

"It's the good time I'm worried about." I wouldn't be so quick to dismiss the leer on his face before the drug hit me. I trusted him about as far as I could spit.

"I told you, you're not my type. Now put the bloody stone around your neck and you'll see I'm mostly harmless."

"Mostly," I muttered.

Kane let out a loud snore and nestled deeper into the sand. He looked so comfortable I wanted to curl up beside him and sleep. I wouldn't though, not here. I didn't believe for a second the demons around the fire were just a bunch of chill stoners. They moved fast enough to do what Sawyer said the last time. They might just be lying —or sitting—in wait for the "fun" Sawyer promised them.

I suppressed a shudder, sucked in a breath and, against my better judgement, put the stone around my neck.

The reaction was instant. Just like the bond with Leo and Dyson, I felt Sawyer's presence and his mood. Right now he was amused at something, probably me and my caution.

I sent him "fuck you" vibes and resisted the urge to poke my tongue out at him.

He grinned and sent thoughts of him touching Leo intimately. Maybe they were memories. Either way, I didn't want to know. I pulled the stone off and tossed it back to him.

Mercifully, the bond was gone again.

"See, nothing to it." He tucked the stones into his pocket. "Be careful for a day or two and you'll be fine."

"Thanks for the warning," I said ironically. "I guess you have to be careful too."

He shrugged. "Yeah, see the sacrifice I made because Cordy wanted to help you out."

I frowned. "Why is that?"

"Why did I make the sacrifice?"

"No. Why does she want to help me?" Wanting to kiss someone and going to a lot of trouble for them were two different things.

"I was asking myself the same thing." He propped his chin on his hands. "I guess she likes you for some reason. Maybe she wants you to understand what went on with Leo."

I blinked a few times. "What do you mean?"

"You're bonded, right?"

"Right," I said slowly. "So what?"

"So he must have had a bonding stone. Or you do and all of this is for nothing." He spread his hands.

"I don't." I tucked my legs under me and thought. "I don't think he did either. He was so certain it was fate." He had the magic sucking stone, but so far I had no reason to think they were related. I decided to keep that information to myself for now.

Sawyer let out a choked laugh. "Leo, the hopeless, fucking romantic." He shook his head. "There's nothing romantic about it. Well, not really. In the wrong hands, bonding magic could be a powerful weapon."

"So what are you saying? Leo bonded with me on purpose?" I didn't believe that. He was as surprised as I was. He firmly believed we were meant to be. I had believed it, too, but now I wasn't sure what to think.

"That, or someone made sure it happened. Although, that someone had to be sure you'd screw each other. It's possible it was meant for someone else, not Leo. You do have quite the collection of cocks."

"Do you have to be so crude about it?" I shifted uncomfortably. Sure my relationships were unconventional, but we did nothing without the knowledge and consent of everyone else.

He grinned. "I wouldn't have thought you were a prude."

I snorted. "I'm not, I just don't like feeling slut shamed. Maybe you're jealous."

I thought he might laugh, but instead he looked thoughtful. "Possibly. Maybe I should gather my own harem and see how I like it."

"Suit yourself." At this point I had more questions than answers. "Do you know why anyone would want me to bond?" That made me more uncomfortable than slut shaming. The idea that someone might have forced this on Leo and I wasn't much better than assault. "And how?"

"A touch with a bond stone would do it," he replied. "Did you bump into anyone in a crowd?"

I thought back to the train. "Plenty." Especially the older woman whose bag almost tripped me. Coincidence? Possibly, but I doubted it. I wished I could remember more details, but I didn't pay her much attention. That was probably the idea. Be forgettable, but do what has to be done.

"As to the why," he leaned back and looked up at the sky. "Maybe Leo paid someone off. He must have been very sure you'd spread your legs."

I didn't rise to his bait. "I'm almost certain he had nothing to do with it. I could have been targeted at random."

"Did I mention how expensive bond stones are?"

"And yet, you have two," I pointed out.

"I know a guy."

"Now you sound like Leo."

Sawyer hissed. "I'm starting to regret helping you."

"Why did you?" I asked. "Really. You don't seem like the type to go out of his way for his sister."

Before he could respond, Kane groaned and sat up.

"Hey, are you—"

I was so focused on him, I almost missed seeing a dark shape leap out of the nearby bushes and bound toward us.

17

THE GARGOYLE WAS SO BIG, I flinched. He growled and threw himself at Sawyer. His friends leapt to their feet with cries of alarm, and scattered.

"Matt!"

He knocked Sawyer back onto the sand and stood with his front paws on the demon's chest.

"I should have know he was your fuckin' dog," Sawyer spat. "Get off me."

Matt leaned down so his face almost touched Sawyer's nose and growled. Deep and menacing, it sent chills down my spine.

"Let him up," I said after a few moments. Of course I had to let Sawyer squirm for a little while.

Matt turned toward me and cocked his head.

"He's a dick, but he's more or less harmless," I assured him.

Matt let out a gusty sigh and climbed off Sawyer. I thought he might shift, but instead he lay in the sand near the demon and rested his head on his front legs. The message was clear, "I'm ready to bite you the moment she says so."

"Lucky that wasn't Nash," I remarked. "He would have ripped your head off and asked questions later." I eyed the bushes as if a dragon might fly out without warning.

"Dyson too." Kane rubbed his head and scooted over closer to me. "Are you okay?"

"Yeah." I gave him a quick kiss of reassurance and searched the bond for Leo and Dyson. Both were groggy, but okay as far as I could tell. I sent them thoughts of me being fine as well. Both responded with relief.

Sawyer slowly sat back up, his eyes on Matt, and brushed sand off himself.

"Hybrids. Why do they always have bad tempers?"

"Maybe it's not them," I suggested. While he scowled, I said, "You called him a dog. Why did the bond not happen with him?" Or Nash for that matter. From what I gathered, dog shifter DNA played a part in the creation of gargoyles and dragons.

"The dog is too diluted in hybrids," Sawyer replied grudgingly.

I nodded, then asked another question. "Can girls bond other girls?" This whole bonding thing would be horribly judgemental if they couldn't.

"Arousal fluids are arousal fluids," he replied. "It's trickier, but possible. Fingers, dildos, etc."

"Right." I swallowed. The visual image made my blood hot.

"You're not bonding my sister," Sawyer said coldly.

"That's up to her," I replied, my tone matching his.

A shadow passed overhead. It blocked out the moon for several heartbeats before it wheeled around.

Sawyer flinched. "Don't tell me, one of your cocks is a dragon?"

"Yeah, but I'm starting to think the biggest cock here here is you," I told him.

He looked down at his groin. "Believe it. Not that you'll ever find out."

I grimaced. "Thank the gods for that."

I rose and waved toward Nash as he flew over again.

He banked sharply and landed a few metres from the fire, scattering sand with his large, clawed feet. He stalked toward Sawyer until he saw Matt lying near him.

"I'm fine, but I don't mind if you bite his head off." I pointed toward Sawyer.

The demon placed a hand on either side of his face. "Hey, I'm attached to my head. Remind me not to help you again."

"It's not the help that's the problem, it's the method," I said. "As a teacher, Nash is well within his rights to eat you." I was only half joking.

Sawyer snorted. "He's not my type, either."

Nash snorted a hot breath out his large nostrils.

"I think the feeling is mutual," I remarked. "But I don't mean the good kind of eating."

"Yeah, I figured." Sawyer moved away from Nash, but the dragon shifter followed him.

"I think he might like you after all." I watched for a moment, then felt Leo and Dyson getting closer. If this place was supposed to be a secret, Sawyer had brought the wrong person here. We wouldn't tell anyone about the place, but we'd know where to find the demon and his friends.

"Someone is coming," Kane said.

Matt rose and padded toward the bushes just as Dyson, Leo, and Blake staggered through and into the clearing.

"I told you she'd be here," Dyson said happily,

"We believed you," Blake assured him. "Well, I did." He glanced at Leo.

"I knew she'd be close, old boy, I was only off by a little bit." Leo sniffed. He stopped and watched Nash stalk Sawyer, a bemused look on his face. "Looks like we got here just in time."

Dyson grabbed my hand to pull me to him and pressed a long, lingering kiss to my lips.

To my surprise and delight, the moment he stepped back, Blake did the same. His mouth was warm and tasted of beer and promise. His hands slid down my sides and around to cup my rear. He drew me closer still and slid his tongue between my lips.

After a long moment, he pulled back and smiled. "I've been wanting to do that for a while."

"Me too," I said softly. "I… I love you as much as the other guys."

"I love you, too," he said softly. "Should we call off Nash, though?"

I looked over my shoulder to see Sawyer stumble back away from the great dragon.

"I suppose so." I sighed. Hopefully he'd learnt his lesson. Don't screw with me. Any woman, really. "Nash, let him be before he wets himself."

"I would never..." Sawyer spluttered, but he looked relieved when Nash stopped and sat in the sand. "Thank you."

"Yeah." I shrugged and looked toward Leo. "We need to talk."

"That sounds ominous," he said, with a nervous glance at the other guys.

I gestured toward the sand and sat cross-legged on the edge of the firelight. When he sat beside me, I told him what Sawyer told me about the bonding.

Every so often, Leo would frown toward Sawyer. But the time I was done, he was scowling.

"It's fate, it has to be, darlin'," he insisted. He looked like a man who had the rug pulled out from under his feet. And then he was rolled up in that rug and tossed off a bridge.

I sighed softly. "Nash was right, it was magic. For some reason, someone needed me to bond."

"Maybe the gods came down to Earth..."

"You believe in the gods?" I asked.

He scratched his head. "Not really, but I'd rather believe that than think someone forced me on you."

I placed a hand lightly on his. "They didn't. I wouldn't have slept with you if I didn't see a future with you. Same for all the guys. Call me selfish, but I want to be with all of you."

Leo leaned in to kiss me lightly. "You're not selfish. We all like this…whatever this is. That doesn't change the fact someone made us bond. How did they even know we were there?"

I gaped. "I hadn't even thought of that," I admitted. Of course, it should have been the first thing to occur to me.

"Is it possible Corinne left us there for them to find?" Leo asked.

"She would never do that," Blake said from where he stood near the fire. He moved closer and looked worried. "Not unless they made her talk."

I shook my head. "Whoever it was was there already, waiting for us."

"Or for him." Kane shot Leo an apologetic look.

Leo shrugged. "Or it's a coincidence and they were just up to some random fuckery."

"I rate the chance of that to be pretty low," I said sadly. "It's more likely they knew where we were the entire time, but they were just waiting for the chance. I thought the drive up here was too easy."

"No one should have known," Nash said with a

growl. He shifted back and now sat naked in the shadows. "I made sure of that."

"Where are Hamish and Ariana?" I asked without thinking.

"They're supposed to be protecting your friend Jess," he said after a moment. "I suspected Zeta might go after her again if they wanted to capture you. It seems as though they've decided on another tactic instead."

"We don't know if they were even involved," Blake pointed out. "Maybe Leo pissed off someone."

"Leo pisses off lots of someones," Leo said. "If they wanted to punish me, there's worse than having me bond a beautiful woman."

"Leo is right," Nash said.

"About pissing people off?" Dyson asked with a smile.

Nash gave a faint smile in return. "About this not being about him."

"So bonding me was to punish Peyton?" Leo asked.

"Possibly," Nash agreed. "But probably not. I think you were coincidental to all of this. If Corinne was involved—" He held up a hand before Blake could protest. "If she was, it's more likely she intended you to bond with Blake."

Blake flopped down into the sand. "You think?"

"There's a chance Peyton and Dyson would have bonded anyway. She might have wanted you to do it first. Maybe she thought she could control Peyton through you."

I snorted. "Not a chance."

"Right," Blake agreed. "She knows Peyton is headstrong."

"Unless she planned to use you as bait," Nash said.

Blake looked as though he might be sick. "I can't believe she'd do something like that." Still, he appeared at least halfway to believing it. "She's my cousin. Surely…"

"Apparently my mother is on the board of Zeta," I said simply. "Just because you're related doesn't mean she can't screw you over." I scooted over closer to him. "I'm sorry. We have no proof she is involved. She might be as innocent as…as…"

"As me?" Leo suggested.

I snorted. "No offence, but that's not a word I'd use to describe you."

"Thank the gods for that." He lay back, his arms over his head. "I'd hate to think you misjudged me that badly."

I laughed softly and leaned into Blake.

"If there's any chance she was involved, does that mean we shouldn't bond?" Blake looked despairing.

Unable to answer, I looked toward Nash. Damn, he was hot sitting there all naked like that. He had muscles for days and a body I didn't want to stop touching for as long as I lived. He was also the rock that grounded and guided us all.

Nash rubbed his chin. "It's possible you shouldn't. If there is some agenda, be it hers or someone else's, we should avoid stepping into the trap. However…" He let the word hang for a moment. "There's no reason not to bond everyone else if you so choose."

My pulse instantly started to race. "Right then." I looked toward Blake, who sat with his head hung.

"It's okay," he said before I could ask. "Go ahead. We'll have time. You shouldn't waste this chance."

I squeezed his hand and looked at Kane. While we talked, Sawyer and his friends, each with a tentative look on their faces, returned to the fire and picked up their hastily abandoned beers.

Kane's eyebrows rose. He looked like a man whose birthdays and Christmases all came at once.

"So, how does this work?" he said slowly. "We make love, right here, right now, we should bond?"

"Exactly," I replied lightly.

He eyed the demons who glanced at us every now and again with interest.

"If they don't like what they see, they can leave," I told him.

Kane smiled and drew me into his arms. He kissed my mouth, long and slow, while his hands worked my shirt up to my neck. He broke off long enough to pull it over my head and tossed it toward Matt.

Matt shifted back into human form and pulled my shirt over his lap. He could try to hide, but I didn't think anyone missed his erection. Good, he'd need it soon enough.

To my surprise, Blake unhooked my bra and slid it down my arms.

"Just because we can't bond, doesn't mean I can't take part, right?" he said softly.

"You absolutely can," I agreed. Oh gods, my blood was on fire already.

Blake reached around to massage my nipples while Kane continued to kiss me.

I tugged on the bottom of Kane's shirt and pulled it over his head. With a grin I threw it so it landed on Leo's face.

"Hey!" He sat up and pulled it off.

I giggled and went back to kissing Kane while he

undid the front of my shorts. I wriggled out of them and my panties went next. In the corner of my eye I caught the demons watching with interest. Sawyer's eyes were huge. Good, let them watch.

I helped Kane with his shorts and lay back to let him lie between my legs. All without our mouths separating for more than a moment.

Blake scooted around and rested on his elbow. He took one nipple between his lips and suckled gently. Matt, who apparently abandoned his modesty, lay on my other side and licked the other nipple.

How in the world I had gotten so lucky, I had no idea. I never, in my wildest dreams, have imagined being the centre of the attention of so many—let's face it—hot guys. If I wasn't me, I would wish I was.

In the meantime, I would just enjoy myself and let the flood of passion grow and wash me away.

Kane finally broke off and moved down my body. He tickled my bellybutton with his tongue, then kissed his way down between my legs. When he finally licked my clit gently, I was ready to come.

I pushed the sensation down for a few moments, wanting to make this last for as long as I could.

Kane's licks because more persistent, faster, deeper. He teased my clit and flicked at my folds. He pressed the tip of his tongue against my entrance and slid inside a little.

I shuddered with the deliciousness of the warmth flooding every bit of me.

He pulled back and replaced his tongue with his fingers.

While he pumped me gently, Blake pressed his mouth to mine. I opened to let his tongue inside, then reached for Matt's cock. It was hot and hard in my hand. With three guys touching me, inside me, I was closer and closer to the edge.

Through the slit in my eyes, I caught sight of Dyson and Leo talking softly. They only exchanged a few words before their mouths met in a heated kiss. That was enough to drive me over the cliff and into a whirlpool that made me cry out loudly. My body rocked against Kane's hand. My hand pumped Matt harder.

"I'm gonna…" Matt panted. "Not like this."

I pumped him one more time, then let him go. He moved away, his teeth gritted.

To my surprise, Kane moved aside and let Matt lay between my legs. With a look of relief, he slid his cock inside me slowly.

"Gods, this is…" Matt breathed.

"It really is," I agreed. My eyes went over to Leo

and Dyson. They had each other's shirts off and Leo's hand was down Dyson's pants.

Dyson caught my look and bit his lip. "Do you mind?" he asked.

I knew if I said I did, they would pull apart and never touch each other again.

"I want to see you two…together," I said in a hoarse whisper. Gods, did I ever.

Leo grinned wolfishly and tugged down the front of Dyson's pants. He bent to wrap his mouth around Dyson's erection.

"Holy gods," Kane breathed. His face was pink, eyes alight with arousal.

Dyson grunted and his hips started to move slowly, pulling his cock in and out between Leo's lips.

Holy gods was right.

"Peyton," Matt panted. "I'm going to come. I want to bond you. I want you…forever."

I turned my eyes back to him. "Come inside me," I said softly. "I want to bond you, too."

He thrust harder and faster then, his cock hitting deeper and deeper inside me.

"Oh, yeah…" He balanced himself with a hand on either side and groaned once, twice. He let out a cry as he came, filling me with hot cum. I came again a heartbeat later, longer and deeper than the first time.

The bond formed immediately, almost faster than with Leo or Dyson. Maybe I was getting good at it or something.

"Whoa." Matt wiped his brow and looked stunned. "I can feel you."

I smiled. "I would think so." Since his cock was inside me.

He grinned. "Yeah, that too." He wiggled his hips and slid free.

"Dude, I'd like to feel the bond, too," Kane said lightly.

Matt rolled aside. "Sorry, mate."

"All good, dude." Kane rolled me onto my side, pulled my leg over him and pressed himself hard into me.

I let out a gasp at the slight sensation of pain, but it was soon replaced by the slow build of another orgasm.

"On one hand, I want this to last. On the other hand, bond," Kane muttered.

"We have all the time in the world," I reminded him.

"Good point." He rolled his hips, pushing himself further into me, then began to thrust with deliberate speed. "Under the circumstances, I'm not sure I could hold it for long anyway."

He nodded toward where Leo was massaging Dyson's balls and sucking him hard. Dyson sat with his head back, ecstasy written all over his face. Through the bond, I felt both of their arousals and every drop of pleasure they were milking from each other. They were as much a part of this as the other guys.

I sought out Nash, who sat away from demons, hungry eyes on me. I knew he also wanted to bond, but he would wait for the other guys. While he seemed to enjoy watching, he had yet to take part in our group adventures.

"Peyton." Kane's voice drew my eyes back to him. "I'm close."

"Let it loose, dude," I said teasingly. I was close again myself.

Kane thrust with frantic speed, then threw his head back. His cry echoed through the night air while his seed rushed into me. This time, I came in perfect unison with him.

The bond took longer to form this time, but when it did, it was as solid as the rest. Maybe the magic was wearing off a little.

"Well, this is cool." Kane cocked his head, as

though conducting a scientific examination or something. "I can sense your thoughts and everything."

"Hopefully not everything." I grimaced.

He grinned. "Okay, not everything. Close enough though. Interesting."

I snorted. "You're such a geek."

"Thanks, love you too." He kissed me before he rolled off me.

I turned my attention to Nash and Blake.

"It seems to be getting harder with each bond," I said. "It might wear off before—"

I hadn't finished my sentence before Nash rose. He rolled me onto my stomach and slammed his cock into me.

I let out a cry of surprise. "Oh gods…sir."

He leaned down to chuckle in my ear and give it a nip. "You make the best noises."

"Of course I do." I cried out again when he drew out, then slammed back in harder than before. Caught between pleasure and pain, my eyes watered, but my arousal rose yet again. With no mercy, not even a little bit, he pounded into me, each thrust firmer and more forceful than before.

He pinned my wrists to the sand and rammed me

over and over until I was ready to scream for him to either stop, or hurt me even more.

His fingers dug into my skin when he came with a ferocious growl and a thrust so hard I thought he might spilt me in two.

Rather than scream in pain, I cried out in pleasure, caught in another orgasm, doubled in pleasure by feeling Dyson come in Leo's willing mouth.

The world disappeared, replaced by pure sensation. No words, only feeling. Only pleasure. Pain. Love. Bond. Relief. Understanding.

Completeness.

I sagged onto the sand and Nash collapsed on top of me, panting and trying to catch his breath.

"That was worth the wait," Nash whispered. "We're one. All of us."

My eyes went to Blake, who sat looking dejected.

"I trust you," I told him.

He blinked and frowned. "What if there's some plan?" he asked, obviously caught between hope and fear.

"We'll overcome it, like we always do."

Nash slid off me and I reached my hand out to Blake.

His gaze went to Nash. "Do you think this is a good idea?"

"You may never get another chance to bond," Nash replied. "But if you endanger her, I will kill you."

"Get in line," Matt growled.

"Behind me," Kane added.

Blake licked his lips. "I want you," he said finally.

"Then take me," I whispered in reply.

He hesitated a moment longer, then pushed his shorts off his hips and drew me up until I was on all fours in front of him. He pressed his heated cock against my entrance.

"Are you sure?" he asked.

"Positive," I replied. I should be exhausted after fucking three guys, but I wanted more, especially seeing Leo and Dyson had swapped places and Dyson was now sucking hard on Leo's cock.

"I brought lube," Leo said softly. He reached for his jeans and pulled out a tube. "It always pays to be ready."

I swallowed as Dyson let Leo ready him. My mouth went as dry as the nearest desert when Leo lay over Dyson and pushed himself into the dog shifter's puckered hole.

Dyson's eyes widened, but he soon relaxed and Leo started to thrust into him.

The position Blake put me in let me watch everything while the bond let me feel it. When Blake slid his cock inside me, I was almost washed away again with arousal.

"I've wanted to do this since the moment I met you," Blake said.

"For me it was when I found out you weren't a baddie," I said over my shoulder.

He chuckled and started to move inside me. Unlike Nash, he was slow and gentle, as if he was scared of hurting me. He didn't seem to be in a rush, even though the magic might wear off. I suspected Sawyer wouldn't let me near the bonding stone again, so if this didn't work…

I glanced over to the demon, to find him locked in the embrace of a woman I hadn't seen arrive. Whatever, as long as he wasn't bothering us.

Blake slid his arms up my stomach and massaged my nipples in time with his thrusts.

"You feel so amazing," he said softly. "Better than I could have imagined."

"You feel pretty good yourself," I told him.

As if that was a cue, he stilled and then came. He gave a few frantic pumps, drawing out his orgasm before he sagged, breathing heavily.

I came once more, rocking my body against him to increase my pleasure.

It wasn't until I came down I realised the bond hadn't formed between us.

"What—"

With a slow build, like a dam wearing down its banks, the bond slowly inched into existence. It crawled as if it was reluctant to exist. As if the magic was all but sucked dry.

It finally became fully formed as Leo let out a cry that let us all know he, too, was coming. I felt his heat flood Dyson's ass. A moment later I sensed Leo's disappointment. No bond formed between them. I hadn't expected it would unless they exchanged places, but I felt bad for breaking the last piece of faith Leo had in the idea of fated mates.

I sagged on the sand, taking Blake with me. I curled us into a ball of arms and legs and contentment.

Still, at the back of my mind I wondered if bonding Blake might be a bad idea.

18

IF I THOUGHT BONDING one or two guys was intense, it was nothing to bonding six. I know, it's my own fault for taking them all on at once, but I couldn't really bring myself to regret it. Sure, it was over-whelming having so many thoughts and feelings in the back of my mind. On the other hand, that was where they stayed. It took no time at all to push them to the back and tuck them away in a little box. It was like shutting out certain sounds. If I let myself become aware, I could tune into one guy over the others, or all of them at once. I hadn't expected to have that kind of control, but I thanked the gods for it.

The guys, however, seemed determined to stay switched on to me and my emotions and needs. I only had to think about tea before someone would bring me a cup. That was cute until three of them had the same idea.

Fortunately when I was in class, they had to focus on their own studies or work.

The CAME campus was totally opposite to the UA or even original AMM campus. Classrooms nestled amongst native trees and bushes. The ground underfoot was as much sand as it was grass and dirt. Most students wore shorts and t-shirts or singlets. Some even wore shoes.

Personally, I was happy in shorts and flat sandals. No tie, no repressed schoolgirl skirts and certainly no jackets. The streak of green in my hair was plain in comparison to many other students. Rainbow or dreadlocks were more common, sometimes both. Yes, rainbow dreads look just as awesome as they sound.

For the most part, the other students gave us a warm welcome. Sawyer and I gave each other the side eye whenever we saw each other, and I avoided his friends and Cordelia. Everyone else was chill though, and free with their offers to share dope.

"No thanks," I said for about the fifth time that day. Even if I was interested in smoking it, I didn't want to put Nash in the position of having to tell me off for it. I had other positions I much preferred to put him in.

"Okay, if you're sure." I didn't know the guy's name, but he gave me a shrug and a smile and went back to sit under a tree with some other students.

I sighed softly.

"You too, huh?" Kane slipped his hand into mine a moment after I became aware of his presence.

"You shouldn't be able to sneak up on me like that," I scolded lightly.

He grinned. "I've been working on my stealth skills. And keeping my thoughts to myself."

I frowned at that. "Should I be worried about you keeping things from me?"

"Only on your birthday." He leaned in to kiss my mouth. "And any time you're with my brother." He grimaced. "Somethings are better not shared, even amongst twins." After all our group intimacy, he was still twitchy about Dyson having any kind of sex life. It was adorably endearing.

"I don't know, you don't seem to mind sharing most other things," I pointed out. "All of you guys are becoming like brothers, in a way."

He swung our hands between us. "Just one big happy family."

"Exactly." It was certainly warmer than the home

life I grew up with. And with a lot more sex and tea. What more could a girl want?

"Luckily you guys don't fight like brothers. Not too much, anyway." Once in a while they'd growl over someone having eaten their yoghurt, or drank the last beer, or wanting to watch a particular movie. Mostly it was in fun, with no hurt feelings.

"Not that you can see," he replied, giving me a half smile.

"Ah, but you forget, I would feel it if you argued," I returned his smile.

"That's true, you would. Fine, we'll behave. Although, if we don't, will you spank us?"

My smile widened. "I'm happy to spank you, argument or not. You only have to ask." I squeezed his firm ass cheek, then smacked my hand lightly across it.

"Remind me to order a paddle next time I'm online." I wasn't sure if he was joking or not.

"Don't forget the blindfolds," I added.

"Of course, we can't forget those. And one of those feather ticklers."

I wrinkled my nose. "If you love me, you won't tickle me."

"I love you very much, but do you know how hard it is not to tickle you immediately after you say that?" He wiggled his fingers in front of my belly.

I squirmed. "Don't even joke. I hate being tickled. I would literally let my tiger loose on you if you do it."

Kane lowered his hand, but his eyes shone. "Noted. No tickling. We'll stick to spanking then."

"Agreed." I chuckled and walked with him, approximately in the direction of the beach. The campus was nestled amongst the trees, but the walk to the sand was short. With windows open, the sound of pounding surf contributed to the serenity of the place.

The dope probably helped.

"I've never been anywhere so chill," Kane remarked. "I mean it's warm, but it's…" He flushed.

"I know what chill means, " I said gently, "but were you reading my mind?" I smiled teasingly.

"Just your mood." He ran his thumb over the back of my hand, back and forth and then in slow circles. "You seem so relaxed here."

I hesitated for a moment. "I am. I think this might be the kind of place I'd like to teach. Everyone is just so laid back, even for Aussies. It's as though no one has a care in the world, even when getting assignments done, or sitting exams. Take the one yesterday for example, no one freaked out. We just went in, did the test and left. Even me. Not one word of complaint, no groaning about being sure they failed." Not that I could see anyway. Even the teachers seemed to enjoy being here.

"I think it's the sea," he said at the same time as I said, "I think it's the marijuana."

I fell against him, laughing.

"It could be both," he conceded. "Or just good teaching. That should help. You knew your stuff, though."

"I felt as though I did. I suppose I should by now, it is third year." Grass changed to sand under my feet. I leaned on Kane while I slipped off my sandals and let the grains fill the gaps between my toes.

I stared out at the wide expanse of ocean spread out in front of us. The sea air ruffled my hair and filled my senses with salt and freedom.

"This is—"

I turned toward Kane as a jolt of pain entered our bond.

"What—" I grabbed at him as he crumbled to the sand. "Kane! *Kane!*"

I felt a surge of concern from the other guys and sent back thoughts of extreme worry and fear.

"He'll be fine."

I recognised the voice behind me, but for a long time, I couldn't bring myself to look behind me. I didn't want to confirm what I had suspected for so long.

"What did you do to him?" I fell to my knees in the sand beside Kane. He lay still, eyes half open, but glazed. I put a finger to his neck. His pulse still beat, but slower than normal.

"He's just out cold. What happens to him next depends on you."

I sucked in a breath and looked up slowly.

"What are you doing here, Mother?"

19

I HOPED she might at least try to tell me she was there to make sure I was okay. That someone else hurt Kane, but she'd help him. Deep down I hoped she'd pull me into her arms, rub my back, and soothe me like a mother should.

Instead, she looked at me with cold eyes, like she barely recognised me. Like I was some kind of laboratory experiment and she was curious about the result. There was no hint of warmth, nothing. She was never loving, but I never saw this clinical side of her before.

"What do you want from me?" I felt vulnerable looking up at her, but I was far from that. I could shift and rip her apart in a heartbeat. She knew that, I saw it in the twitch at the side of her mouth. She also knew I wouldn't. In spite of never having been close, she was still my mother.

"I want you to come with me. We have much to learn about the bond." She nodded to someone behind me.

I turned my head just enough to see Corinne. She wasn't what took my breath away. That honour went to Blake, who walked beside her.

"I'm sorry," he mouthed.

What the fuck?

I probed the bond to gauge his mood, but somehow he blocked me out. All I could feel was that he was alive. That wouldn't last long if he really betrayed me.

"This works best if you don't fight us." Lucinda—I couldn't think of her as my mother right now—was all business.

"Did it cross your mind we might have come willingly, without you harming Kane?" I asked coolly. "We'd also like to learn about the bond."

Surprise was the first hint of emotion to cross her features. Of course it didn't occur to her. Ruthless people assumed ruthless tactics were needed for everything. Gods forbid they'd resort to not being assholes once in a while.

The look was gone before I could blink and her mask of ice was back.

"Then we won't have any trouble. Bring the shifter." She turned away and started toward the carpark.

For a moment I thought about setting my tiger or gargoyle loose from my tattoos and letting them rip her to pieces. I curled my hands into fists, but uncurled them. I wasn't lying when I said I wanted to understand the bond better. If I had to play along for a while, then so be it.

Between them, Corinne and Blake supported Kane and carried him toward a white SUV. White, as if somehow my mother was totally innocent.

I trotted to catch up with her.

"Are you really working with Zeta?"

She pulled a key out of her pocket and pressed the button to unlock the SUV.

"Zeta aren't the enemy," she said as she pulled the back door open and gestured for me to climb inside.

"Like hells they aren't," I growled. "Have you got any idea what they've done to me?" My eyes narrowed. "Of course you do, you know all about the attack on the AMM campus in Sydney. I told you. But you knew before that, didn't you?"

She hesitated. "That was an unfortunate misunderstanding—"

"*Misunderstanding?* Fucking hells, people *died!*" I gaped at her. Who was this woman? Had someone stolen my mother's face? "Paranormals died. I almost died! I had to kill to save myself and people I loved!" I was almost shouting now. Tears streamed down my face at the memory of the attack. I wasn't proud of anything I had done, but I had no choice.

"Did you know they put me in a lab and wanted to use me for breeding?" I planted my hands on my hips to keep from wrapping them around her throat.

"That was my fault." Her voice lacked any emotion.

"Your fault?" My stomach lurched. "You arranged to have that happen to me?"

"No," she replied. "I should have explained the purpose you were made for."

What the absolute stone cold fuck?

"Made for?" I echoed. "I'm a person. I decide what happens to my life. I'm not a piece of technology, to be tweaked and thrown around."

She sighed. "Get in the car. I'll explain everything when we get there. You will understand fully and when you do, you'll happily cooperate."

"Doubtful," I retorted. "Right now I trust you

as far as I can throw you." I frowned. "Actually if I use magic, that would be pretty far. Forget throwing, I don't trust you as far as I can spit you." I was babbling, but mostly because the rug had been yanked out from under me, yet again. This, though, this was different. I both had no choice, but also a bad feeling that if I got into the car, my life would never be the same. Whatever happened now, there would be no coming back from.

Lucinda shrugged. "That's up to you, but if you won't trust me, then trust your father. He adores you. Do you think he'd let you come to any harm?"

The mention of him left me breathless. "What has he got to do with this?"

Lucinda quirked an eyebrow. She actually seemed amused at the question. "Why everything, of course. You didn't think I was doing all of this behind his back, did you?"

I shook my head slowly. "I have no idea." Honestly I couldn't be sure if she was lying right now or not. My father and I were close. If he was involved then maybe she really wasn't so bad. The idea burned inside my head, but I came to no conclusions. I needed to see him, to speak to him, for myself.

"I didn't," she said firmly. She moved aside to let Corinne and Blake heft Kane into the car.

I shot them both a dirty look. Corinne looked as cool and calm as ever, but Blake at least looked uncomfortable.

"He did well, wouldn't you say?" Lucinda nodded toward Blake. "Your bond will be very helpful."

I shot her a scowl, then turned it on Blake. "If you fucked me over, I'll never forgive you."

"You should get in the car," he said without meeting my gaze.

Yeah, fuck you too, I thought. Tears prickled at my eyes again. I climbed into the car and scooted over closer to Kane.

"Did you get it?" Lucinda asked as she climbed into the front passenger seat.

Corinne held out her hand, palm up. She uncurled her fingers and I gasped. On her palm, she held the stone Leo stole from Zeta, the stone which sucked magic from witches and wizards.

"How did you—"

"He should have kept it in a better place than his pants pocket," Corinne said.

I looked into her eyes, but saw no sign of regret. She played me and felt no remorse whatsoever. Had she played Blake as well, though? I still didn't want to believe he would betray me. Especially choosing to bond me when he knew this would happen. Had he known? Was he as complicit as Corinne and Lucinda? If he was, I was taken in, hook, line, and sinker by that curly hair and those dimples.

My heart ached.

"It's good to have Zeta property back in our possession." Lucinda took the stone from Corinne and tucked it away in her pocket.

I consoled myself with the knowledge that at least it wasn't a bonding stone. That only made me feel better until I realised Lucinda probably knew about those already.

"You arranged it so I'd bond Leo," I said, directing the question at either of them.

"The demon wasn't part of the plan," Lucinda said. "You weren't supposed to miss your train."

I frowned. "But I was with—"

Blake slid into the seat on the other side of Kane.

"You," I finished. "That was meant for you."

He flushed slightly. "I didn't...it wasn't..." he stammered.

"Of course it was," Corinne said sharply. "You were away from Matt, Nash, and Kane. The timing was perfect, until you missed the train." She sounded as if she blamed me for that.

"Well, lucky for you we bonded anyway," I snapped. "You must be delighted I fit into your plans after all." I directed my icy gaze to Blake.

"It's not that simple," he muttered.

"Why don't you enlighten me then?" I suggested.

"When we get there," Lucinda said.

Corinne started the car and we pulled out of the carpark. In the back of my mind, I felt the guys looking for me. I assured them I was okay, but then pushed them aside. As much as I wanted them to come after me and Kane, I didn't want them to get hurt, or worse.

I took hold of Kane's hand and held it loosely in my lap. At any other time, he'd have his fingers between my thighs in moments. Now, he just lay still, face pale, breathing slowly.

"It is just tranquilliser?" I asked. "If you've done him any lasting damage, I'll be much less cooperative."

"He'll be fine," Lucinda said dismissively. "He'll stay that way if you don't do anything stupid."

"When have I ever done anything stupid?" I asked ironically. "Surely I was raised better than that." Putting the blame on her if I did anything rash might be childish, but it felt good. That was until she responded.

"I would have thought so too, but it seems we have some gaps to fill."

"Are you regretting not having me raised in a lab?" I asked. I meant it as a joke of sorts, but once the words were out, I wanted to know the answer.

"Perhaps that would have been best," she said, as if it would have been the most normal thing in the world. "Your father didn't want that for you. In retrospect, I might have insisted."

"Gee, thanks. Don't do me any favours, will you?" I wanted to curl up in a tiny little ball and cry. Even though she was always distant, both physically and emotionally, she did give birth to me. Surely some part of her cared about me? Loved me even? This woman in the front seat of the car didn't seem to have a drop of feeling for me.

Lucinda let out a frustrated exhale. "It might have been a favour, Peyton. Then you wouldn't be so ignorant about so many things. You wouldn't feel the need to fight me. Don't think I don't know what's going on in your mind. It's written all over your face and I know you better than you know yourself."

"Says you," I muttered. "I don't think you know me at all. It's not like you took the time."

She was unfazed. "That might be right, but your friends here will help to fill in the gaps."

I bared my teeth and Corinne's back, but she was focused on driving. I couldn't bring myself to look at Blake. He could certainly tell Lucinda a lot about me.

I gritted my teeth and forced a breath in and out. "So where are we going?"

"You'll see."

"When do we get there?"

"If you start asking 'are we there yet,' it won't end well for your shifter friend," Lucinda growled.

"I wouldn't dream of it." I slumped down in my seat and held Kane's hand tighter. I planned to do just that, if only to get under her skin. I wouldn't risk Kane's hide just for my own amusement. That would take petty a step too far and achieve nothing.

"Good. Now you can be quiet and wait patiently while we travel."

"I thought you knew me," I muttered. If she really did, she would know I didn't do patience well. For Kane, I would keep the peace. For now.

Deep down, in the very back of my mind was the all too real fear we might not get out of this alive.

2 0

WE PULLED UP AN HOUR LATER. I might have expected an abandoned warehouse, or some sort of industrial looking complex. Instead, we drew through the gates of a huge beachside mansion. I wouldn't be surprised to see a Hemsworth jogging around the grounds, or swimming in one of the enormous swimming pools. My inner kid delighted at the sight of not one but two waterslides which spiralled down toward one of the pools. Real ones, not created by magic.

"Do we get a cocktail upon entry?" I tried to keep my awe out of my voice, but I was pretty sure I failed.

"Once you've heard what I have to say, you can have whatever you want," Lucinda replied.

"Freedom?" I asked.

Her hesitation was all the answer I needed. The gate clanged shut behind us with a finality that made my heart sink. Realistically, I could shift and leave at any time, but my relationship with my mother would be over. Was it already? I could be wrong, but I'm pretty sure her behaviour wasn't normal for a parent. Not a loving one anyway.

I willed Kane to wake up, but he was blissfully asleep, even as a giant descended the front steps of the house and hefted him over his shoulder. Okay, I don't mean a literal giant, but he was at least seven feet tall and almost as wide. I might have been impressed, except the whole working-for-my-potentially-evil-mother thing. All right, maybe I was a little bit impressed anyway. He'd probably be able to walk around with a Hemsworth under each arm.

"It'll be okay." Blake went to touch my arm, but I jerked away. The look I gave him should have melted stone, but probably looked like I needed to use the toilet.

"None of this is okay," I snapped. "I should have known I couldn't trust you or your cousin."

He looked stung, but nodded. "I understand. So will you. Very soon."

"Sure." I turned my back on him and marched up

the steps behind Muscles. He didn't even look like he broke a sweat.

"Put him down on the couch over there," Lucinda instructed.

"Aye." Muscles nodded and did as he was told. Did I catch a hint of a Scottish accent in the single word he'd spoken?

He lowered Kane to the couch and tucked a cushion under his head like the owl shifter was some kind of doll.

"So what are you?" I asked. Muscles or no muscles, I still had sufficient power to hurt him. I craned my neck to look up at him and arched an eyebrow. "Demon? Blue whale shifter? Oh wait, let me guess, cyclops?"

Muscles smiled in response. "Name's Macintosh." Yes, that was a Scottish accent, but from the way he turned and walked away, all the answer I would get.

"Well, he's a friendly fellow," I said sarcastically.

"I apologise for not rolling out the red carpet," Lucinda said dryly. "I'll be sure to be more hospitable next time."

"Skip it," I replied. "There won't be a next time." I glanced around and tried not to be impressed by the opulent surroundings. "This doesn't look much like a laboratory."

"No," she agreed. "That's downstairs. If you're cooperative, we won't have to take you down there." The look she gave me convinced me she meant every word.

I flopped down beside Kane and winced when he bounced slightly.

"Sorry, babe," I muttered. Louder, I said, "If he doesn't wake up soon, it's going to put a dent in my goodwill." That was already pushed to the very edge.

"It won't be much longer," Lucinda sat in a chair opposite me, looking like a cat curling themselves, waiting to pounce on unsuspecting prey. "We have time to talk."

I glanced toward Corinne and Blake, who both hovered near the door. Corinne's face was unreadable, but Blake seemed anxious. So he should.

I looked back toward Lucinda and crossed my arms. "I'm listening. You have until he wakes to convince me. Otherwise I'm taking Kane and getting the hells out of here."

Lucinda rolled her eyes as if I was a stubborn three year old who stomped her foot to get her way.

"By now, you've learnt of the existence of hybrids," she stated.

"Yeah. Thanks for the warning I might shift someday." I wasn't going to tell her what I could shift into. If she didn't already know, she wasn't going to find out from me.

"It wasn't assured. You're one of the first ever second-generation hybrids. For all we knew, you'd lack magic, much less the ability to shift. You could have been a mule, magically speaking."

I blinked. "I beg your pardon?"

"A mule," she repeated. "A species, when bred back onto itself, can become sterile. At some point the tinkering might produce—" she grimaced with distaste, "—regular humans."

I snorted. "That would have been ironic." Of all the witches in the world, Lucinda was one of the most powerful. For her child to be lacking in magic would have been a huge slap in the face for her.

"Indeed. Your friend Jess is a good example. Very embarrassing for her family." Lucinda clicked her tongue. "Still, she'll be taken care of."

My jaw dropped. "You can't mean…"

Lucinda gave me a dry look. "We don't condone murder. Besides, her children may be a throwback. We'll be watching carefully. Our little lesson last year will have ensured she keep her mouth shut. She knows our reach is long."

"You had her kidnapped?" I asked, horrified.

"Not me, personally. The decision was made by

someone else in the organisation. I was only aware of it after the fact. Still, it served its purpose."

"To catch me. Why didn't you just *talk* to me?" I asked.

Lucinda sighed. "I would have preferred that. Others in the organisation tend to get overly dramatic about certain things. I'm also aware some individuals might have convinced you Zeta meant you harm."

I lowered my arms and sat forward. "An agent named Fitz tried to *rape* me. What conclusion would *you* draw from that?"

Lucinda flinched. "There are bad apples in every bunch. That particular one was taken care of—"

"Yeah, I killed him. I also met a girl there who said forced impregnation like that was normal."

"Some girls don't understand what Zeta is trying to achieve." Lucinda's tone was as stiff as her back.

"That includes me. Why don't you enlighten me?"

Lucinda sighed and waved toward Corinne. "Get us some tea."

Corinne hurried away to do as she was told, like a good little lackey.

Bitch.

"As you know, paranormals are superior to normals," Lucinda declared.

My eyebrows shot up. "Do I know that? I don't recall being tranquilised, kidnapped, assaulted, attacked, or threatened by any normals recently. Paranormals—sure. I'm really starting to think paranormals suck."

"Some paranormals—"

"Oh please," I interrupted. "Don't start with hashtag not-all-paranormals. They were acting for you, with your blessing. I only have your word for it they acted without your full knowledge. Maybe you wanted Fitz to rape me. To *break* me."

Lucinda shifted in her chair. Blake made a choking sound. I didn't even glance at him.

"Was that the plan?" I asked insistently. "To break me down until I had no fight left? To drive all of the spirit out of me so I'd go along like the dutiful broodmare you seem to think I was born to be." I bit back a sob.

"If that was what it took," Lucinda said softly.

I gaped at her. "Why? Because you knew I'd never go along with any of this?"

"You always were a stubborn brat."

Her words left me breathless for a long moment.

"Just like you," I said finally. I remembered something else then. "You took part in the breeding program. Did they *make* you take part?"

She averted her eyes. "I was young. I didn't understand the significance."

"And so you decided it was fine to put me through that?" That revelation cut me through and through, more than anything she could ever have said. She experienced the nightmare, but threw me in anyway. What sort of mother does that?

"Paranormals are dying out," she said finally. "We need to increase our numbers. In a generation, there will be only a few thousand left. Normals outnumber us terribly already."

"I wonder why," I said sarcastically. "Maybe we should stop killing each other."

She hesitated. "The Academy of Modern Magic was an unfortunate casualty in the power struggle between Zeta and the Paranormal Council. The council doesn't agree with our methods."

"Neither do I," I replied stiffly.

"The council would prefer we all die out," Lucinda said as if I hadn't spoken.

"I'm with them." In the corner of my eye, I caught Kane twitch.

"Nevertheless, you were born to help grow the population of paranormals. Now we understand more about the bond, we can extend that to all of our breeders. Running away, for example, will be more difficult."

I glanced toward Blake. He was listening as intently as I was.

"Is that why you wanted me to bond him?" I jerked a thumb toward Blake. "So he could keep track of me?"

"Exactly. In addition, when you two breed, he'll be in tune with your cycles. All the better to impregnate you at the right time."

"What makes you think I'll let him lay a hand on me again?" I asked. I swallowed to keep from throwing up on the expensive-looking carpet.

Lucinda sighed. "You can't really want paranormals to go extinct?"

"That was all you wanted me to understand, wasn't it?" I asked. "That and you think I have no choice in the matter. You'd let him force himself on me."

"There's always a choice," she said. "You bonded several other paranormal men. Any of those would be suitable." She waved toward Kane. "Him, if you must. If you can't choose, we'll choose for you."

"As long as I have a pile of babies, you don't care who fathers them."

"Precisely." She looked relieved, as if she was

finally getting through to me. "I blame myself for not explaining this to you sooner. You've wasted a good few years. No matter, you can catch up." She waved a hand as if it was all that simple.

"You're sick," I stated. "Fucked up in the head. If I didn't know better, I'd think you believed all of this shit."

Anger flashed in her eyes. "Don't take that tone with me, or I'll knock you flat myself." She drew magic from the environment around us and held a glowing ball on her hand.

I drew magic of my own, but she reached into her pocket with her spare hand and pulled out the black stone.

"Try it. I'll suck you dry before you take another breath," she hissed. "Then I'll throw you into a cell and leave you to the mercy of the worst of Zeta. By the time they've done with you, you'll beg to be allowed to do your duty." Her eyes were filled with cold fury. I never saw this side of her and it terrified me.

I believed everything she said. Any hope I had that she might care about me deep down fled. She was nothing but a block of ice. Ruined and determined to let me suffer the same fate as she had.

Twisted and fucked up didn't come close to covering it.

"Peyton?"

I jerked my head to the side at the sound of a new voice.

"Dad?" I let the magic go and reluctantly looked away from Lucinda. It wasn't the sight of my father that left me gasping for breath. It was the young woman beside him.

She looked a lot like me.

21

SHE DIDN'T HAVE the green streak, but the rest of her hair was the same colour as mine. Her face was the same shape and her eyes—

Her eyes were the same shade, but they were so full of loathing. I would have taken a step back if I was standing.

"So this is my sister." She walked toward me, hips swinging with each slow step. She was the big cat, I was the tiny mouse.

I held back a squeak.

"Peyton, this is Rebecca." My father's voice was filled with regret, but I hardly dared to take my eyes off her to look at him.

"Hey." I smiled as warmly as I could manage. "It's

nice to meet you. I heard a rumour you existed, but I wasn't sure if it was true or not."

Rebecca bared her teeth, but the growl was aimed at Lucinda.

"I'm the family secret," she hissed. "The disgrace."

"Really?" I asked lightly. "I could have sworn that was me." I gave my mother a sweet smile. I wasn't sure if Rebecca was my ally or not, but she seemed to loathe our mother as much as I had come to in the last couple of hours.

Rebecca laughed, a bitter, cold sound. "You're the one they kept. They left me to be raised by Zeta doctors."

I nodded. "I thought I recognised that bitter expression." I had seen it on Nash and Matt. Whatever childhood they had was tainted by the sick idea that paranormals were superior and needed to be preserved at all costs. I would never understand how my parents didn't think the price was far too high.

For the first time since he'd entered the room, I looked at my father. He seemed to have aged since I saw him last. He looked tired, his face lined and pale.

"So, you knew about all of this Zeta stuff too?" I asked.

He flinched. "In the early days, yes I did. I left. We left. Or I thought we did." His gaze settled on my mother. "I was told Rebecca was dead and they'd never touch you."

Lucinda met his gaze, unwavering. "I did what I had to do."

"You're fucked up!" Rebecca shouted, all but drowning out Lucinda's last couple of words. She lunged at her.

My father was quicker. He grabbed Rebecca's wrist and pulled her back.

She hissed and growled like a cat with its claws caught in a trap, but she only struggled against him for a few moments. Then she sagged.

"She deserves to die," Rebecca said, her chin tucked into her chest.

For a moment I thought my father might agree. Instead, he said, "She did what she thought was best."

I blinked. "Do you know what happened to me?" I gestured toward Kane. "To him? To everyone else I care about?"

Kane's legs moved, but his eyes stayed closed. I felt around in the bond. He wasn't entirely out now, but he was going to keep pretending he was. I sent thoughts of approval. For his own safety, he should keep still for as long as he could.

"I know," my father said softly. "I didn't know until a few days ago. Any of it." He looked at Rebecca with cautious affection. I suspected only his inno-cence kept her from ripping off his head. What had the doctors at Zeta said she was? Oh yes, a chimera. A dangerous one at that.

"Well, aren't we a dysfunctional family," I said ironically. "How many babies has she had?" I nodded toward Rebecca.

Lucinda snorted. "None, she's too unstable."

"Unbroken too," I observed. Damaged by her upbringing, yes, but she obviously still had her will intact.

"Stubborn," Lucinda said. "The bond will help with that."

Rebecca made to attack her, but again our father held her back.

"You really mean to do that?" he asked. He looked disgusted, but like a man who knew better than to argue. Lucinda would do as she pleased. If not her, then someone else from Zeta.

"Now we know exactly how to do it, and have one who can spell the stones." For a moment I thought Lucinda meant me, but she nodded toward Corinne, who reentered the room carrying a tray.

"I would hazard a bet your young lover could do it too." Lucinda waved toward Blake. "Perhaps I'll have him bond Rebecca."

Blake's eyes widened. An hour ago, I would have defended him, but now I had no idea what he might be capable of.

"I'll tear off his head if he comes near me," Rebecca said, her voice low and dangerous. "Both of his heads."

Lucinda clicked her tongue. "It's past time you learnt obedience." She raised her hand and drew in magic. Before anyone could move, she wrapped a thick tendril around my father's throat.

"Don't!" I was out of my seat before I could stop myself. "Leave him alone!"

His face turned pink and he put his hands up to his neck.

"You both need to learn what happens if you don't behave," Lucinda said coldly.

My father dropped Rebecca's wrist and fell to his knees. Only when they touched the floor did Lucinda release the magic. He slumped forward, coughing and gasping for breath.

"You're not going to win wife or mother of the year," I told her. "In fact, I think that's very good grounds for divorce."

"Perhaps you need another lesson." Lucinda raised her hand again.

"No! No, leave him alone." I stepped between

them as Rebecca helped him to his feet. "This is all about you and me. Let them both leave and I'll do whatever you want." Gods, what was I saying? It didn't matter, I meant it. If I had to go along with her disgusting plans to give my sister and father a life, then so be it. They both deserved to be free of Lucinda.

Lucinda regarded me coldly, as though deciding whether or not she believed me. Finally, she nodded.

"Very well. Corinne, see them out. Peyton, I need to be certain you'll do as you say you will."

"I said I would, didn't I?"

"People say many things they don't mean," she replied coolly. "Hold out your hand."

I hesitated, then slowly did as she asked. I thought I heard a choked protest, but I couldn't be sure who it was from. Maybe my father had regrets, maybe Kane was worried, maybe Blake still cared about me on some level.

Lucinda pulled out the black stone from her pocket. Without a second's pause, she touched it to my palm.

A heartbeat, two, three and all the magic inside me slithered up into my hand and into the stone. Not a drop remained. I tried to draw, but couldn't even feel the magic I knew was around me. I immediately felt bereft, empty. I wasn't a witch anymore. I swallowed back a sob.

A flash of triumph crossed her features.

"Peyton—"

I glanced at my father as Corinne herded him and Rebecca toward the door. His expression made my heart skip. It wasn't one of a man whose daughter gave everything to keep him safe. Oh, there was regret, but he looked like a man who didn't like the plan, but was glad it worked. He set me up. Lucinda had never had any intention of killing him.

"I can still shift," I reminded them all.

"But you won't," Lucinda said. "Your sister and your shifter lover's lives depend on you doing as you're told." She nodded toward my father who took Rebecca's wrist again, but this time as a prison guard, not a caring father or husband trying to protect his wife.

"Divorce is still an option," I called out to him before the door closed on them.

I didn't see the slap until the side of my face stung. My head snapped back on my neck and I almost fell on my ass. Only by windmilling my arms did I keep my feet.

"Have some respect," Lucinda hissed.

I cupped the side of my face with my hand.

"Respect is *earned*. You've done nothing to earn it. Quite the opposite."

Lucinda raised her hand, but that was the only indication I had that she was doing magic until Kane started to thrash on the couch. His hands curled like claws and scratched at his neck. His eyes popped open and his face turned red.

"Paranormal shortage," I reminded her. "And if you kill him, our deal is off."

Kane gasped for air and Lucinda lowered her hand.

"Macintosh, take the shifter to one of our *rooms*."

I hadn't seen the man enter the room, but he swung Kane over his shoulder like he had earlier and carried him toward the door.

"Don't worry, you'll be right beside him," Lucinda told me. "The bond will ensure you feel everything he does, or which is done to him. When you step out of line…"

Even without magic, the bond still held. She was right, I would know if she hurt him. Gods, how had I done this to us?

"If you behave, he'll be allowed to visit you. I hear he quite enjoys having an audience."

I flushed. "The others will come after me," I told her.

"It's up to you to keep them away. Otherwise—" She waved a hand in the direction Macintosh had taken Kane.

I licked my lips. "They're pretty stubborn."

"Then your shifter better enjoy pain, because he'll be getting used to it." She took a step toward me. "It doesn't have to be that way. This could be an enjoyable experience for all of us." She moved away from me and toward Blake. She ran a hand down his cheek, over his chest and down toward his groin. "I might even have more children myself."

Blake's eyes widened. He let his control slip for long enough for me to feel him through the bond. He was trying hard not to flinch away from her.

I might have laughed, or felt sorry for him, but he made his bed. He could lie in it, even if that meant lying with her, too. The idea was revolting, but it still wasn't the worst thing I heard all day.

"I'm sure Blake would enjoy that," I said. Why not twist the knife a little? "He seems to like fucking for the sake of Zeta." I curled my lip at him. "Like a dutiful breeding bull."

He looked away, so I couldn't see his response.

Lucinda chuckled and patted his groin. "That's what I like to hear. Now, Blake, take her up to the rooms. She'll need her birth control implant removed. Again. That can't be done until morning. Make sure she has food and doesn't shift. I would tell you what would happen if you don't, but you know if she does, she'll kill you first."

He swallowed and nodded. "Yes, ma'am, I know she will," he agreed.

"Darn right I will, but it's nothing he doesn't deserve." I gave him an ice cold look, but my heart ached. I had cared about him as deeply as the rest of the guys. His betrayal cut me deeper than if he'd shoved a sword between my ribs.

"Yes, yes, enough of that." Lucinda waved us away. "Just see she's comfortable and behaves until she's ready to breed. That's our top priority here. I will be checking up."

"Yes, ma'am." Blake gripped my arm tight and pulled me toward the door.

"I know how to walk," I growled. "I don't need you to touch me."

"I'm just doing what I'm told," he replied.

"Yeah, that's what I don't get. Why you're on her side."

"I'm on the side of paranormals surviving." He opened the door and pushed me through.

"Me too," I agreed. "Me, Kane, and my sister. You, your cousin, and my parents can go to hells."

22

I FLOPPED down on the bed in the corner the moment Blake shut the door behind us.

"Okay, what the fuck is going on?" I fixed him with a steely gaze.

He looked around the room, ran a hand along a wall. "Kane is in the room beside this?"

I felt for him through the bond and nodded. "He is, but he's pissed off. I can't guarantee he won't peck your eyes out the next time he sees you. And Corinne."

Blake pulled a chair away from the table on the other side of the room. "I'm going to assume we're being watched and listened to."

"Whatever." I grabbed up a pillow and hugged it to myself. "I don't care if they hear. What could you say that would make any of this better? Or worse?" I shouldn't suggest the latter. I'm sure my mother could think up a few ways.

"I didn't mean to hurt you," he said softly. He glanced around again, then let a hint of his feelings filter through the bond. Regret, anxiety, love, fear.

I turned my face away. "You shouldn't have lied to me." The words were harsh, but they had a new meaning now. I understood. At least, I hoped I did.

"I had no choice." He sat forward, hands on his knees. "I had to do what was right for all paranormals."

"Corinne too?"

His lips drew tight. "She believes in Zeta's cause."

I exhaled through pursed lips. I hoped she really was on our side. I genuinely liked her, or I did. Now, she was as bad as my mother. I felt for Blake. He was walking on a tightrope between two sides. One he believed to be right, the other that would kill him if he didn't toe the line. At least for now.

That didn't mean I wasn't still mad at him. He scared me. I honestly thought he went over to the evil side. I couldn't think of it as anything else. Not even the extinction of all paranormals justified forcing young women to have children.

"What about my father and Rebecca?"

"Today was the first time I've seen either," Blake replied. "Your father seems conflicted. I'm sure your mother will keep him and Rebecca in line."

"That's what I'm afraid of." I wasn't sure how conflicted he was. He seemed as deep in this as Lucinda. Rebecca, on the other hand, was as much a victim in this as I was. More so. I could just as easily have lived the same life she had.

I rested my chin on the top of the pillow. "You know I've going to have to escape, right? I know what I promised my mother, but I can't stay here and pop out babies. Even if they have cute, curly hair."

He smiled out the side of his mouth. "I wouldn't expect anything less, but it'll be harder without your magic."

Tears prickled my eyes again. "I'll find a way to get it back."

"And if you don't?"

I paused. "I can be badass without it. They can't take away my ability to shift."

"Not yet," he agreed. "I'm sure they're working on it."

My lips trembled. The idea I could be stripped of every ability that made me paranormal was enough to make me weep or scream. Maybe both.

"I might have babies without abilities if they do," I said finally.

"That would be ironic," he agreed. "After all the trouble they've gone through to convince you to stay."

"That would be so fucked up I could almost laugh at the idea." Almost. Mostly I just wanted to burn the whole house to the ground.

"Yeah, but they're working hard on doing the opposite. I suspect that's what your mother took all that magic for."

I frowned until I understood his meaning.

"You think Zeta wants to make normals into paranormals?"

"It certainly seems like something to try," he replied carefully.

"Then they wouldn't need to breed us." They'd create a shit ton of other problems instead. A normal who woke up one day with the ability to shift or do magic, could cause havoc while trying to figure out what was going on.

"No, but they might start with children too young to understand."

I shuddered. "I thought my mother's job was to stop normals from finding out about paranormals. This would have the opposite effect."

"Only if the children were raised amongst normals," Blake said softly.

My mouth dropped open and I gaped for a solid minute.

"She would do that, wouldn't she?" And Corinne and my father would help her. "I need to get my magic back before she gives it to some unsuspecting normal."

"How are you going to do that?" he asked.

I slumped and held the pillow tighter. "I don't know." I scanned the room. If a camera was tucked away in a corner, I couldn't see it. Or a microphone. Maybe the wall was a one-way window and Kane was watching our every move. And maybe no one was watching, they just wanted me to think they were.

"Is there any chance you could get me some chocolate?" I asked after a few moments.

Blake smiled. "Probably. This place seems to have everything."

"Yeah. Pool, spa, resident evil witch," I said bitterly. "You know, you should probably leave, before you end up dead." I made it sound like a threat, but it was a warning. If Lucinda or even Corinne decided he couldn't be trusted, he'd lose his magic and then his life. Once his usefulness was done, so was he.

"I won't leave until my job is done," he replied. "And right now that means watching over you. What kind of guard would I be if I left?"

We'd long since established that he wasn't cut out to be any kind of guard, so I had to bite back a smile.

"Suit yourself." I shrugged.

"I'm sure you'd prefer not to have a replacement," he said, his voice low. "Macintosh, for example."

I shuddered. "He'd tear me in two. Don't even say things like that."

The hint of a smile on his face faded. "Yeah, sorry. Nothing about this is funny. I just…I'm not good at knowing what to say at times like this."

"Yeah, me either. Except maybe, 'I'm a hybrid, get me out of here!' I suspect Lucinda wouldn't be swayed by that."

"Probably not," he agreed. "Maybe you should get some sleep. I'll keep watch."

I nodded and lay back on the bed. "No taking advantage of me while I sleep." I shook a finger at him.

"I wouldn't dream of it," he replied. A smile tugged at the corners of his mouth. "Actually I would and I have, but I won't."

"Until you have to." I pulled a blanket up to my chin.

"Yeah, until then." He crossed his arms over his chest and exhaled out his nose.

I felt his conflict through his bond. On one hand, he didn't want to be part of Lucinda's plans. On the other, we loved each other. None of us had ever really talked about children, but the possibility for them in the future had always been in the back of my mind. Any child I had would be loved by all the guys. No matter what they went through, they'd have a father they could go to for advice or permission.

"Whatever happens, you'll have to keep doing what you're told," I said, my eyes peeking over the top of the blanket. "Like a dutiful lackey."

"I don't want to—"

He was interrupted by the door opening so hard it slammed against the opposite wall. Corinne stood in the doorway with a specimen jar in one hand.

I sat up and shuffled back against the wall.

"What do you want?" I asked, when Blake apparently had no words to greet her with.

"You might think I betrayed you—" She started.

"That's exactly what I think," I snapped. "Have you told them every detail about us and our lives?"

She shrugged unapologetically. "What was neces-sary for them to know."

"You arranged for me to bond." I fixed her with a steady look.

"Yes. I told them where I was dropping you off and they arranged the rest." Her expression was so cold I almost couldn't recognise her.

"Why?" I asked. "Can't you have all the little babies for them?"

She flinched. Apparently I hit a nerve.

"I can't have children, or I would. Paranormals don't deserve to die out. We can't afford to be selfish right now. The future of—"

"Fuck the future." I flung off the blanket and got to my feet. "You can't possibly think this is okay?"

She stuck out her chin and thrust the specimen jar toward Blake. "Someday you'll understand."

"What is this for?" Blake took the jar and peered at it as though it might explode in his face. After what we'd seen, it wouldn't have surprised me if it had.

"Lucinda wants you to bond Rebecca," Corinne said coolly. "I convinced her you wouldn't force yourself on her, so she relented and gave me that. I'm sure you won't have any trouble filling it." She shot me a sarcastic smile.

"How do you propose to get his cum inside my sister?" I asked. Even if Blake wouldn't force her, others might.

"You let us worry about that," Corinne told me. "Your mother can be very persuasive. Failing that…" She shrugged.

"This has nothing to do with Rebecca, or breeding paranormals," I said sharply. "You want to punish my sister because of me. Because of things you think I've done."

"Your sister is wild and out of control. Bonding is a last resort. If she lashes out at anyone after that, she will have to be taken care of."

"She's not an animal," I growled.

"She's a shifter," Corinne replied. "A hybrid. You've seen first hand how some of them are little more than beasts. Your sister is one of the worst. A failure."

"I've also killed," I pointed out.

"But you're able to keep yourself under control," Corinne pointed out. "Blake and I both witnessed that."

My mouth twisted. "And if you hadn't?"

She didn't reply.

"The day we met. You knew I was coming, didn't

you? You and Blake were placed there to pretend to help me escape?"

"It wasn't entirely coincidence," she agreed. "But Fitz was out of control. We were sent to take charge in case he decided to kill you before you could shift. Or worse."

"Gods forbid he managed to get me pregnant and spoil your plans," I said bitterly.

"Believe it or not, we don't want you broken. We'd prefer your complete cooperation. That would be best for all concerned. You could get a great deal of pleasure out of it."

"Believe it or not, I do realise there's more to life than sex." No, really, it's true.

"There doesn't have to be," she said in a tone that would have sounded reasonable had she been talking about anything else. "Lie back and enjoy the ride." She actually looked wistful.

"Because you wish you could do that?" I frowned. That didn't jive with the kickass woman I knew. Or —thought I knew. Hells, she could be the kind of woman who wanted to be barefoot and pregnant, fawning over some guy who went to work in a bank every day. There's nothing wrong with that, of course, but it wasn't what I wanted for myself.

Her expression tightened. "Just use the jar. I'll be

back in half an hour to collect it." She turned on her booted heel and slammed the door shut behind her.

"We really need to get out of here," I said. And get Rebecca and Kane out with us, before it was all too late.

Blake sighed and turned the jar over in his fingers. "Yeah. Yeah we do."

23

"COME ON." Blake waved me over to the bed.

I eyed him, but took the few steps closer. He lifted up the blanket and climbed inside before moving over to make room for me. Something in his eyes made me slip in beside him. He tugged the blanket over us, but left a big enough gap to let in some light.

Tongue between his lips, he unscrewed the lid of the specimen jar.

"You can't really mean to—" I stopped short when he peeled back the lid. There, taped underneath was a small, black stone. "That can't be..."

"It's not the same one your mother took," he whispered. "It looks like a piece of it, or a smaller version."

I leaned back. "If that's the case, whose magic is in there? Or is Corinne up to something else?" I wouldn't rule out my mother's involvement either. Or my father for that matter.

"I don't know. The question is, do we try to use it to give you your power back?" He picked at a corner of the tape with his fingernail.

"The bigger question is, can we trust Corinne or not? One minute we can, then we can't. I don't know what to think now." I liked roller coasters as much as the next person, but not like this.

Blake scratched his head. "She's risked a lot to get this stone to us."

"She said to use the jar," I murmured. "Anyone listening would think…" I might have been clutching at straws here. I wanted to believe she was on our side, if only for Blake's sake.

"She was still in on the bonding," I said finally.

Blake's teeth flashed white in the under-blanket gloom. "She might not have had a choice, but she would have known it was something we wanted."

"That's true." I sighed softly. "There was no reason for her to reveal herself to Zeta when we would have chosen that for ourselves. We *did* choose that." I placed a hand on his rear and gave it a playful squeeze.

"Yes, we did. Now, are we going to try this?" He pulled away one side of the tape and left the stone to dangle.

"Maybe you shouldn't touch that," I advised. "It might suck away your magic instead." I wished I could assume that wasn't the intention. Why suck Blake's magic away though? Unless they knew which side he was on.

I shook my head slightly and reached for the stone. Whatever the intent was, I wouldn't let him risk himself for me.

Tentatively, I placed the tip of my little finger on the stone. For a breath or two, nothing happened. Then, with a rush of heat, a trickle of magic surged into my finger. It travelled into my palm and up my arm. From there, it spread around my body like a familiar warmth I hadn't known I'd missed until now.

I could feel it calling out to all the natural elements in the environment around me. I felt Kane in the room beside us. The bond with Blake strengthened, when I hadn't even noticed it having been weaker.

The stone went cold.

"I have my magic back," I said in wonder. "The amount I had before I was ever near the bigger stone." Maybe Corinne sucked it from the other stone somehow. I hoped so, that would mean it was mine to begin with.

Blake grinned. "She should be back soon. Then we can get out of here." He screwed the lid back on the jar and tucked it under the pillow. "No offence to your sister, but my cum is all for you."

I laughed softly. "Just as well." My laughter faded and I snuggled into his arms. "Should we just try to get out now? No offence to your cousin, but I'd prefer to be long gone from here. If she's going to keep pretending she's on their side, it's better if we don't involve her any further."

"Yeah, that's true." Blake looked thoughtful. "Maybe you should hit me over the head and run."

I frowned. "You want to stay?"

"No, but I want you to be safe." He pressed a soft kiss to my lips.

"I'm not leaving without you," I said firmly. "All for one and one for all, or whatever the musketeers said."

"Okay, you win." He sounded relieved. "Is Kane ready?"

I felt through the bond. Kane was sleepy, but trying to stay alert.

"He'll have to be. Let's hope we can leave without

having to kill anyone." As long as we snuck, we might just manage it. If not…

We'd cross that bridge when we got to it.

"All right." Blake took my hand and helped me back out of bed.

His hair was messy in the most adorable way. Mine was probably messy like I'd spent the last decade without a hairbrush. This was no time for vanity, I reminded myself, while I patted it back into place. What? A girl has to have some pride, even if she looks like she went backward through a bush.

Blake unlocked the door and eased it open. Lucinda must have assumed it was enough to keep me in. If Blake was on her side and I had no magic, she might be right. With magic, I could pick that bitch in a heartbeat. The lock, I mean, although let's face it, "bitch" applied to Lucinda as well.

The corridor outside our room was dark. No one stood outside Kane's room. In theory, it was easier to lock a shifter in, but that depended on the shifter. Nash would have clawed the door out of the way without a thought.

I felt through the bond for him and the others. They were getting closer, but were more anxious with each passing minute. I sent thoughts of being fine and Blake being fine, too, but it did nothing to assuage their fears.

Men.

Blake put a hand on the lock to Kane's room. The click as it unlocked echoed through the corridor. It couldn't have been that loud, but it seemed deafening.

I flinched and pressed myself against the wall while Blake eased the door open.

Kane leapt out and swung a fist at Blake's face. He connected hard enough to knock Blake back a few steps.

"You fucker," Kane growled. "We should have known you're on Zeta's side. I'm going to knock your fucking block off." Before he could advance on Blake, I grabbed his arm and held him back.

"It's okay, he's with me," I whispered as loud as I dared.

Kane froze. "I heard him downstairs. Him and his cousin."

"They were pretending," I said quickly. "Like you were pretending to sleep."

Kane frowned, but his body relaxed slightly. "Are you sure?"

"I'm sure of Blake," I said firmly. "The jury is still

out on Corinne. Come on, we need to get out of here before anyone comes."

Kane nodded. "Sorry, mate. I just assumed…"

Blake rubbed his jaw. "Yeah, it's okay, mate."

"You two are starting to sound like Leo," I joked.

"I'm not sure if that's a good thing or not." Kane took my hand and we walked silently toward the stairs.

"Better than getting all bossy like Nash." I smiled.

Kane snorted softly. "Nah, I'll leave all the leader-ish things to him and you."

"Me?" I started to say something else but stopped to listen. "I think I hear someone." Considering the amount of noise we had made already, that likely went both ways.

"It might be Corinne," Blake whispered.

It might, but it might also be someone else. I doubted my parents, sister, and Macintosh were the only people in the building. Just because I hadn't seen or heard anyone, didn't mean they weren't here. Gods, there could be rooms of witches locked away.

"They're getting closer," Kane said.

"Can you shift? You could get out of here now. Or at least check the coast is clear."

"I can try." He let my hand go and without a sound, shifted into his adorable—I mean kickass—

owl form. His clothes fell to the floor. I grabbed up a shirt and his underpants, while Blake tossed his pants, socks and shoes back into his room. We couldn't very well leave them lying around to be found.

He flapped through the darkened corridor and landed on the top of the bannister leading downstairs. If he was an actual owl, he would have had my blessing to leave a big poop on the fancy timber railing.

Hells, as a shifter, he had my blessing, but he didn't do it. Of course not, he had more class than the people holding us here.

He shuffled his wings and sent a warning through the bond. Whoever was coming, it wasn't Corinne.

Shit.

"Time to go invisible." I grabbed Blake's hand and formed a bubble around us. He could do that for himself, but I might lose him in the darkness.

"I know you're here, Peyton." Lucinda's voice drifted up the stairs just before she appeared. "I'm disappointed your guard turned out to be such a failure, but I anticipated that. He can't keep you both invisible for long, you know."

I let out a soft breath. So she had no idea I had

my magic back. I could just reach out with a tendril and give her a shove…

She moved away from the stairs.

Bugger.

"It's unfortunate you chose to break the promise to stay and do your duty," she went on. "I should have raised you better." She stopped and seemed to sniff the air. Was it possible she was also a hybrid of some kind? The thought didn't occur to me before, but I was almost certain she wasn't.

"You don't need to respond, I can hear you thinking."

I was very certain no paranormal had that kind of ability, outside a bond, and we definitely weren't bonded. Well, outside the parent slash child bond, but that was diminishing by the moment.

I tugged on Blake's hand and pulled him closer to the stairs.

"You failed to make your owl invisible," Lucinda pointed out.

I hoped she missed him in the dark, but evidently I was wrong.

She drew in magic and threw a ball of it toward Kane. It struck him and knocked him backward in a shower of feathers.

"Kane!" I shouted before I could stop myself.

Lucinda spun and aimed the magic right at me.

I dropped into a crouch and the magic sailed over my head.

"That was too close," Blake said in my ear. Before I could stop him, he rose out of the bubble, fully visible for anyone to see.

"Leave her alone," he growled. He drew his own magic and went to throw it at Lucinda. Before it even left his hand, she blasted him square in the centre of his chest. He was knocked back off his feet. He hit the wall hard and slid to the floor with a thud.

"You bitch!" I cried out.

"Well, well, well." Lucinda circled slowly. "You have your magic back. It seems I have more than one traitor in my midst. No matter, she'll end up like her precious cousin."

I glanced toward Blake and bit back a sob. He lay still.

I rose and let the magic go. "The only other one who is going to die here is you," I said, my tone dangerously cold. I forced back tears. I couldn't lose focus now. Blake might be dead, Kane too, but I had to deal with Lucinda.

"You can't kill her," a new voice spoke from the

top of the stairs. I hadn't heard Rebecca approach, but she was here now.

"Says who?" I asked icily.

"Says me," Rebecca replied. "I won't let you." She curled her hands into claws and started forward.

I took a step back. It was a lucky thing I did, or I might have been stepped on by Rebecca's enormous feet.

No, I'm not big-feet shaming my sister, she shifted into what I assumed was her chimera form. Her head was now that of a lioness. Another head that looked like a goat stuck out her back. Her tail looked like a series of snakes, whipping back and forth.

She looked pissed. No, that was an understatement, she looked like fury itself. And every drop was directed at Lucinda.

"Let me guess, you didn't want me to kill her because you want the honour?" I asked. "I'm not sure that's the answer. We could take her back to the Paranormal Council and they could—"

Rebecca swiped a clawed foot at Lucinda's midsection.

Lucinda ducked away and threw a ball of magic at her elder child.

"Or not." Now I *wanted* to be seen, in case Rebecca accidentally clawed me. I sensed she didn't mean me any harm, but she almost hit me with her swaying tails once or twice. All of her attention, however, was on Lucinda.

I considered helping her, but at that moment Blake groaned. That was followed immediately by a heavy thud right above my head.

"Looks like the cavalry has arrived."

The thud was followed by a scraping and tearing on the roof. The ceiling started to break apart and rain down plaster on our heads.

Half a breath later, a dragon nose poked through a hole in the ceiling.

"Oh, hey Nash," I said lightly. "You're just in time."

He snorted softly and ripped the hole wide enough to let Dyson and Leo drop down beside me.

"Peyton, darlin', I was wondering where you got to. Remind me never to ride on the back of a dragon again." Leo gave me a quick hug and Dyson did the same a moment later.

"Where's Matt?" I asked at the same time Dyson asked, "Where's Kane?"

"Matt is alerting the council," Leo said.

"Kane was near the stairs." Torn between looking for the owl shifter and checking on Blake, I settled for the latter when the guys ducked past Rebecca's tails and hurried to search.

By now, Lucinda was backed up against a wall. I guessed I was right, she wasn't a hybrid. Right now, she just looked like a scared woman. I almost felt sorry for her. Almost.

"Rebecca, listen to reason," she called out in a thin voice. "What would your father think?"

"He seemed to think the same as you did," I said. I kept my distance from Rebecca, but stepped closer to Lucinda while inching toward Blake. I poked around in the bond in the hope of rousing him a little more. "Why should we give either of you mercy?"

Blake's eyelids flickered.

"We are your parents," she insisted. She tried a different tack. "Your father wanted the best for you. He spoilt you, I suppose, but you know he adores you."

"He has a shit way of showing it," I replied. I flinched as the ceiling behind me collapsed a little further and Nash dropped to the carpeted floor.

Lucinda's eyes flicked between the hybrids.

"This is Nash," I said conversationally. "He's not happy about your behaviour either. He'd prefer not to bite your head off, but he will if he has to. Right, honey?"

Nash bobbed his head.

"I…" Lucinda swallowed. "Nash is not his real name—"

"I don't care what his real name is," I said firmly. "He can call himself Bob Down if he wants to." I understood then. Lucinda was one of the people who arranged for hybrids like Nash and Matt to be raised the way they were. They ran from her and others like her. It must be taking everything inside Nash not to shred her like cooked chicken. He wouldn't though, unless it was a last resort. He was better than that. Better than her.

Rebecca, apparently tired of all the chatting, let out a growl and resumed closing in on Lucinda. She moved up the corridor enough to let me get to Blake.

"Blake?" I put a hand on his shoulder. I didn't dare to shake him, in case I hurt him worse.

He groaned and opened his eyes a crack. "I'm all

right. I think." He winced as he raised one arm, then the other and wriggled his fingers. "Nothing's broken except my pride."

"Can you move? We should give these guys some space." I helped him to his feet. He staggered the few steps to the top of the stairs and sat down out of sight.

Just as he did, Leo and Dyson appeared from the corridor on the other side of the stairs.

"We found Kane." Dyson's voice broke on as he spoke his brother's name. "He's…"

My heart sank. The words choked my throat. "He can't be."

Dyson blinked. "Oh no, he's not dead. He has a broken arm and probably leg. We'll need some help to get him out of here."

I stared. "Later, remind me to sock you for scaring me like that."

Dyson gave me a half smile, half grimace. "Yeah, sorry."

"Mate, don't fuck with a lady's… Don't fuck with a lady." Leo clapped him on the back. "Or a chimera. Bloody hells, she's impressive. It must run in the family."

I smiled. "Probably."

My smile faded when I turned to see Lucinda

pinned between two huge talons. Her face was pale, eyes wide with terror.

I felt nothing, not even a hint of sympathy for my egg donor.

"She's not a good person," Blake said.

"No, she's really not, but—" I winced and turned my face as Rebecca drove a talon right through one of Lucinda's eyes. Blood squirted out all over my sister and the carpet. In moments, the expensive pile was slick and red.

"Yuck," Leo groaned. "Have I mentioned I'm really not good with gore?"

"Yeah." I leaned away from Blake so I didn't get him when I vomited all over the floor. "Neither am I."

Rebecca shifted back into human form and fell to the ground, sobbing and rocking back and forth.

I hesitated for a moment, then wiped my mouth and went to crouch beside her. Slowly and tentatively, I put an arm around her. She was covered in blood, slick with it. I had to remind myself not to think too hard about whose it was.

"I'm sorry she did all of that to you." Truthfully, I suspected I hadn't scratched the surface of whatever "all of that" might entail. Maybe I never would.

"I've been wanting to do that for a long time,"

Rebecca whispered. Her face was so pale I thought she might be in shock. I couldn't blame her for that. I was pretty shocked myself.

"Yeah, I don't think you're alone in that."

"No, she's not." Nash was back in human form and wrapped in someone's jacket. I thought it might be Leo's. "The council is coming. They'll search the place and figure out what else was going on here." His expression was just this side of a thundercloud ready to burst.

"They're here," Matt's voice came from the stairs. He appeared with a grim look on his face to match Nash's. "They've been trying to find this place for some time." He took one look at Rebecca and pulled off his shirt to offer it to her.

I took it with a nod and wrapped the fabric around her shoulders. After a moment, she tugged it the rest of the way on. Blood soaked into the fabric, but at least she had some modesty.

I rose and moved closer to Matt so I could speak without Rebecca hearing. "My father is here somewhere too. He knew."

Matt gave a curt nod. "I'll let them know."

"Corinne is on our side," Blake said from his spot against the wall.

"We think," I said with a nod.

"She's been keeping the council apprised as best she could," Matt assured us. To me, he said, "There's someone downstairs to see you."

I nodded. "I think we'll need some help to get down. Some more than others."

Dyson and Leo carried Kane between them. His arm and leg were both at odd angles and I felt his pain through the bond now he was closer, but he was alive, thank the gods.

Nash and Matt helped Blake and Rebecca. I walked behind them, not touching, but near enough to know the other was there. We missed so much already. I hoped some day she'd be ready to handle having a crazy sister who had so many guys in her life. One day at a time on that score.

We passed a handful of what I assumed were representatives of the council. They were talking in low voices, several to women in various stages of pregnancy. Each woman had that haunted look in their eyes, but at least now they were free to raise their children without Zeta taking them and experimenting on them. That so easily could have been me. My heart went out to each of them. Doing their so-called duty took its toll. They would need a lot of support in the coming years.

"Peyton!" Another familiar voice greeted me

when we stepped out the front door and Ariana threw herself into my arms.

"Ariana, why are you here?" I hugged her tightly.

"Hamish and I were on our way to school when we heard what your mother did. We might have followed Nash." She shot him a sweet smile.

He responded with a frown, but said nothing. What could he say? We all got out alive and more or less in one piece. Without my mother and with the help of the Paranormal Council, hopefully Zeta's breeding program was at an end.

I had a suspicion Zeta itself would go on in one evil form or another, but if they stopped trying to impregnate me against my will, I would appreciate it. I'd quite like a quiet life for a while. I had studies to finish, a job to find, and a life to make with my guys.

"I have great news, too," Ariana said. "Guess what?"

"You're crazy and I'm not?" I replied automatically. "Wait, we all know that isn't true."

Ariana grinned. "No, you're just as crazy as I am. But it's better than that. The Academy of Modern Magic has a new campus! It's up in the—"

I only half listened while we walked out to waiting cars. With any luck, the new campus would be safe for the rest of the school year and the years to come. Maybe I would teach there some day.

Nash slipped a hand in mine and drew me to him as we walked.

Matt took my other hand in his.

I sent them both thoughts of love through the bond. They sent it back. My heart was so full I thought it might burst. This was the best part about the future. The bit I was looking forward to the most. Spending time getting to know and love all my guys.

I don't know how I got so lucky, but I was going to spend the rest of my life enjoying every single second of it.

EPILOGUE

"You look hot, sir." Nash in a suit was enough to make my mouth dry. The sight was almost as good as Nash *out* of a suit.

"I hate this shit," Nash grumbled. He sighed out his nose and cupped my cheek. He ran his thumb over my lips. "I know it's your graduation rehearsal, but this formal crap sucks. I'd rather be alone with you somewhere."

Before I could respond, his phone rang. He looked at the number and scowled before he put the phone to his ear.

"What?"

No one could ever accuse Nash of wasting words.

His scowl deepend.

"What is it?" I whispered.

Nash shook his head. "You already owe me about four favours, Evans," he growled.

He listened for a moment.

I strained to hear, but couldn't catch more than a word or two. Something about car full of paranormals, and Zeta. I grimaced.

"Fuck." Nash sighed. "Where?" A moment later, he added, "Yep."

He ended the call. He was almost smiling. "How would you like to skip the rehearsal and tear off some Zeta heads?"

I grinned. "Let's do it."

THANKS FOR READING.

Come back to the Zetaverse for a whole new adventure in Summoned by Fire, book 1 of Harmony's Magic.

Yes, I know the epilogue is intended to draw you into the new series, but if you liked this one, then you'll LOVE Harmony.

Try it. I dare you.

ABOUT THE AUTHOR

Maggie Alabaster is the pen name of Australian author Mirren Hogan. Mirren lives in NSW, Australia with one spouse, two daughters, dog, cat, and countless birds.

Sign up for my newsletter! Sign Up!
    Join my reader group! Join here!
    Follow me on Bookbub! Click here to follow me!

Summer's Harem

Book 1: Shimmer

Book 2: Glimmer

Book 3: Flicker

Complete collection

Short reads

Taken by the Snowmen

Jingle All the Way

Also by Maggie Alabaster and Erin Yoshikawa

Caught by the Tide

Book 1–Pursued by Shadows

Book 2 Pursued by Darkness

Book 3 Pursued by Monsters